Cooper Brock leaned forward and Serena automatically pressed her spine against the ornate wood chair. "Is this why you have avoided me all month?" he asked in a husky voice. "Because you see me as the enemy?"

"How could I avoid you?" she asked irritably. "You were everywhere I turned."

"You refused every invitation I offered."

"You mean every indecent proposal," she snapped.

She sensed the savage hunger beneath his veneer of civility, and yet the man managed to make the promise of a one-night stand sound like a sacred experience. She rejected him outright but he didn't give up. If anything, his invitations became more extravagant and imaginative. It had become a game between them.

There were moments when she wished she could entertain the idea. A few times when she wanted to forget about this revenge. Just for one night. Break free from the dark emotions that suffocated her. Explore the attraction she shared with Cooper. Enjoy life.

That was when she knew Cooper Brock was very dangerous. Not once had she considered stepping back from her vengeful plans until she met him. It worried her. She didn't know why she felt that way. Did it mean her drive was weakening? Or that her desire for Cooper was stronger?

The world's most elite hotel is looking for a jewel in its crown and Spencer Chatsfield has found it. But Isabelle Harrington, the girl from his past, refuses to sell!

Now the world's most decadent destinations have become a chessboard in this game of power, passion and pleasure...

Welcome to

The Chatsfield

Synonymous with style, sensation...and scandal!

With the eight Chatsfield siblings happily married and settling down, it's time for a new generation of Chatsfields to shine!

Spencer Chatsfield steps in as CEO, determined to prove his worth. But when he approaches Isabelle Harrington of Harringtons Boutique hotels with the offer of a merger that would benefit them both...he's left with a stinging red palm-shaped mark on his cheek!

And so begins a game of cat and mouse that will shape the future of the Chatsfields and the Harringtons for ever.

But neither knows that there's one stakeholder with the power to decide their fate...and their identity will shock both the Harringtons and the Chatsfields.

Just who will come out on top?

Find out in:

Maisey Yates—**SHEIKH'S DESERT DUTY**
Abby Green—**DELUCCA'S MARRIAGE CONTRACT**
Carol Marinelli—**PRINCESS'S SECRET BABY**
Kate Hewitt—**VIRGIN'S SWEET REBELLION**
Caitlin Crews—**GREEK'S LAST REDEMPTION**
Michelle Conder—**RUSSIAN'S RUTHLESS DEMAND**
Susanna Carr—**TYCOON'S DELICIOUS DEBT**
Melanie Milburne—**CHATSFIELD'S ULTIMATE ACQUISITION**

8 titles to collect—you won't want to miss out!

TYCOON'S DELICIOUS DEBT

BY
SUSANNA CARR

First published in Great Britain 2015
by Mills & Boon, an imprint of Harlequin (UK) Limited,
Eton House, 18-24 Paradise Road, Richmond, Surrey, TW9 1SR

© 2015 Harlequin Books S.A.

Special thanks and acknowledgement are given to Susanna Carr
for her contribution to *The Chatsfield* series.

ISBN: 978-0-263-25835-6

Harlequin (UK) Limited's policy is to use papers that are natural,
renewable and recyclable products and made from wood grown in
sustainable forests. The logging and manufacturing processes conform
to the legal environmental regulations of the country of origin.

Printed and bound in Great Britain
by CPI Antony Rowe, Chippenham, Wiltshire

Susanna Carr is an award-winning author known for her contemporary romances. Readers throughout the world find Susanna's stories a delightful escape that has often helped them through difficult times. Reviewers frequently describe her work as 'fun', 'sexy' and a 'must-read'. When she isn't writing, or spending time with her family in the Pacific Northwest, Susanna enjoys reading romance and connecting with readers online.

Visit her website at www.susannacarr.com

Books by Susanna Carr

Mills & Boon® Modern™ Romance

Prince Hafiz's Only Vice
Secrets of a Bollywood Marriage
Her Shameful Secret

One Night With Consequences
A Deal with Benefits

Beasts of the Desert
The Tarnished Jewel of Jazaar

**Visit the author profile page at
millsandboon.co.uk for more titles**

To editors Pippa Roscoe and Carly Byrne, with thanks.

CHAPTER ONE

THE NATURAL BEAUTY of the Algarve was lost on Cooper
Brock as he strode across the well-maintained beach, his
handmade shoes kicking up the white sand. Anger rolled
through him, pressing against his chest, ready to tear free.
He ignored the heat blistering through his black business
suit as he scanned the people sunbathing.

Where was she? Cooper clenched his teeth as he studied a group of women frolicking in the ocean. Where was
Serena Dominguez, the woman who had tormented him
for the past month? The moment they met four weeks ago
at a charity dinner in London, Cooper had pursued her
relentlessly, enjoying the thrill of the chase. But what she
did today changed everything.

She had no right to invade his territory. Cooper wanted
to bellow his displeasure until it rang in the air. Victory
had been in his grasp. After two years of incredible patience, he had almost closed the deal that had eluded the
Brock empire.

And he had done it within the law. It was like winning
a bar fight with one arm tied behind his back.

The Alves property had represented more than a major
deal for his family's business. It had been the one prize
his father had not been able to claim. Finalizing the deal

today would have proven once and for all that his methods were better than Aaron Brock's.

Serena had interfered with more than his business, Cooper decided as his mouth settled into a grim line. This deal would have brought him a sense of deep satisfaction. The achievement would have blunted the edges of the restlessness he could no longer banish.

He came to an abrupt halt when he heard the throaty laugh over the ocean waves and the snatches of the desultory conversations. The sound gripped him as the sexual hunger scorched through his veins. He knew it belonged to Serena. He hadn't heard it before—it was one of the many things she wouldn't share with him—but somehow he knew. Cooper changed directions and marched to the oversize blue umbrella at the very back of the beach.

Cooper halted his pursuit when he spotted Serena Dominguez. His heart lurched and he hunched his shoulders as if he had taken a fist into his stomach. He raggedly drew in a breath, wishing he didn't react like this every time he saw her.

He decided it was safer if he focused on her feet as he approached. The gold chain around her ankle caught his attention as it gleamed under the sunlight. It was the kind of gift an infatuated man gave to his woman. He didn't want this woman to be claimed by another and fought the need to rip the anklet from her.

Cooper's gaze traveled along the length of her strong and toned legs to the white bikini bottoms that scandalously clung to her hips. He closed his eyes and swallowed hard as the hunger for her tore through him. He forced his eyes open and determinedly stared at Serena's profile as she ended a call.

He was disappointed that her large sunglasses hid most of her face. He stared at her high cheekbones, full lips and pointed chin. Serena Dominguez was more than just beautiful. Her sensual grace left him spellbound.

She tossed her cell phone down and reached up to smooth the wavy dark brown hair that cascaded past her shoulders. Her sudden stillness was his only indication that she saw him.

"What are you playing at, Serena?" he said in a rough whisper.

"*Olá*, Mr. Brock," Serena said, her Brazilian accent making his name sound like a caress of a bold lover. "What brings you to Portugal?"

"Drop the innocent act. I don't have time to play games."

"How very unusual," she said as she removed her dark sunglasses and set them on her head, pushing her hair back. "You live for games."

The shade of her eyes reminded him of his favorite gold tequila, only her gaze packed a stronger punch. He also noticed her tight and polite grins had disappeared and were replaced with a wide and brazen smile. He had wanted to see her smile at him. He had ached for it. But not like this.

"I was supposed to close the deal today on the Alves land," he said as calmly as he could while the anger whipping through him collided with his ferocious lust for her, "and I find out that you stole it from under me."

"Stole?" She clucked her tongue at the word as her eyes glittered. "Careful, cowboy. I'm not a thief."

The way she said it suggested he was the one who couldn't be trusted. That was ridiculous. "How did you pull this off? I know you're some sort of financial genius, but you don't have the money or the connections to make this kind of deal."

She splayed her arms out. "I don't need any of that when all I have to do is bat my eyelashes and smile."

And wear very little, Cooper decided as his gaze drifted

to her voluptuous breasts. The delicate bikini top faithfully outlined her curves as her tight nipples pressed against the thin white fabric. She may as well be sunbathing topless.

He cleared his throat but his voice was gruff as he replied. "If you think I'm going to let you take what is mine and walk off into the sunset, you don't know me very well."

She laced her hands behind her head and he knew the movement was not as casual as it appeared. It was designed to divert his attention. "You would be surprised at how much I know about you."

"Don't play with me, sweetheart," he warned quietly as he dragged his gaze back to Serena's eyes. "What do you want with this project?"

"Nothing. I simply wanted to intercept the deal. How does it feel not getting what you wanted? To fail? To have something you need snatched away. It must rub at you." She pursed her full red lips with false concern before her mouth widened into a bitter smile. "Don't worry. It will only get worse."

"If you wanted to get my attention, you've had it since I first met you."

Serena arched one eyebrow as her smile faded. "It's not your attention I want. I thought I made that very clear."

"Who are you kidding? You can't keep your eyes off me." It was one fact that had kept him sane all these weeks.

"Only because I've learned not to turn my back on a Brock," she said as she reached for her drink.

"Well, don't leave me in suspense. You must want something very badly from me to go through all this work."

She took a sip of her cocktail and licked the moisture from her lips. He wanted to capture the tip of her tongue with his own so badly that he almost missed her answer.

"How is it that you have pursued me for the past month but you don't know anything about me?"

He crossed his arms and braced his legs as he towered over her. "I know all that I need to know. You're smart, sexy, and you keep your distance from me because you know I would actually make you feel something."

Amusement flickered across her face. "Keep telling yourself that if it makes you feel better." She paused and tilted her head. "That's it? That's all you know?"

"What else do I need to know?" Other than the magic word that would get him into her bed, but she wasn't going to share that.

"This should not surprise me at all. It's exactly how you make a business deal. No research. It's a visceral decision for you," she said with a mix of distaste and wonder. "You decide you want something and you go after it, so sure that you will succeed."

"It works for me." He didn't see any need to apologize for it.

"If there are any obstacles, all the better. It makes the win sweeter. Any enemies blocking your way and it makes the game more interesting for you."

Cooper narrowed his eyes. "You know this and yet you are in my way."

"You keep pursuing me without learning anything about me." She paused to take another sip of her drink. "But I have learned so much about you."

"I'm touched," he replied as he watched a drop of condensation fall from her glass and onto her chest. He watched it glide between her breasts, his hands itching to rub it into her oiled, bronzed skin. He wanted to follow the lazy path of the droplet and catch it with the curl of his tongue. "You could have saved yourself the work and asked me directly," he bit out as the lust pounded in his blood.

"But you wouldn't have told me what I wanted to know," she said in the soft, lilting voice that always made his body harden. "Would you have told me that you just made a lucrative deal with the Australian mining company? Congratulations, by the way."

Cooper squashed the start of surprise and jutted out his chin. "How do you know about that? It hasn't been announced."

"Or that you're secretly negotiating with the telecommunications conglomerate in Zurich?" Her dark eyelashes fluttered. "It's a gamble, but I think you will pull it off like you always do."

Cooper's eyes narrowed. He had just visited Zurich this weekend and both companies had been very careful not to have that information leaked. "Where did you hear that?"

"Around." She gave a delicate shrug. "And I know you wouldn't have told me what you won at the Chatsfield poker tournament in Las Vegas last year."

Cooper frowned. "No one knows…"

"That you won a twenty-five percent stake in The Harrington from John Harrington, Jr.?" she finished for him. "Don't worry, my lips are sealed."

Cooper stared at Serena. No one knew he had the shares. *No one.* John Jr. definitely didn't want anyone to know. How had she found out? And did Serena know why he needed the Harrington shares so badly?

He had underestimated her. The woman had single-handedly uncovered his secrets. How many more did she know? And what did she plan to do with it? "Why have you been acquiring all of this information about me?"

She yawned and stretched, arching her back. He held himself very still as he watched the sensuous roll of her torso and the tantalizing thrust of her breasts. "I guess I just find you so fascinating. Growing up in such wealth and privilege."

Cooper pulled at his shirt collar. "Serena…"

"After all, you have been living the life I should have had." Her eyes dulled with cold anger. "You dismissed the opportunities that should have been mine."

"What are you talking about?"

"Ask your father," Serena said in a hiss as she glared at him. "Ask him about Felipe Dominguez. Fourteen years ago he bankrupted my father's company. Destroyed it."

His skin prickled as a cold sensation settled in his chest. The name wasn't familiar but that sounded like something his father would do. "If that happened, it has nothing to do with me."

"Right," she said in a drawl. "You only benefited from it. You lived off the spoils of war. But it has nothing to do with you."

He raked his fingers through his short hair and gave a huff of frustration. "What does this have to do with the Alves land?"

"Everything," she replied flatly. "I'll tell you more tonight. Meet me at the grill for dinner here at The Harrington. Let's say around eight? Where are you staying?"

Cooper stared at her as he shook his head. No way. He would not let her dangle pieces of information in front of him. Put him off and have him heel to her commands. Cooper swiftly moved forward and clamped his hands on the armrests of her chair.

He reluctantly admired Serena's composure. She didn't jump or scream. She didn't curl into a protective ball or push him away. Serena unflinchingly met his gaze as if she already knew what his next move was going to be.

He leaned in, so close to her that the tropical scent of

her suntan lotion hit him in the back of his throat. "Tell me everything now," he ordered. His voice was harsh as his anger started to slip but Serena obviously didn't give a damn.

"I wish I could but I'm working right now."

She was such a princess, Cooper thought with disgust. A spoiled socialite who got whatever she wanted the minute the idea popped into her head. She thought the world revolved around her. Cooper fought the urge to grab her out of the chair and toss her into the ocean. "Serena, I swear…"

"You really have no choice in the matter."

His fingers curled around the armrests until his knuckles whitened. "I always have a choice. What I don't have is the time for this."

"Time?" She scoffed at the word. "Cowboy, I've been waiting fourteen years for this moment. Of course, I thought it would be with your father, but you'll do."

He'll do? He slowly released the armrests and rose to his full height. He needed to keep his distance before he followed his impulse and wrapped his hands around her slender neck. "I don't know where you get the audacity…"

"We will discuss the details over dinner." She waved her hand as if she were dismissing a servant. "It's the only time I can fit you in but you may not have the stomach for all the gory details. It is Aaron Brock we're talking about."

He swore this woman had a death wish. He wouldn't allow people to talk about his family that way, not even this temptress who had invaded his dreams. "My father is a respected businessman throughout the world. No one has a bad thing to say about him."

"No one said a bad thing because they feared him," she said. "I'm happy to tell you all that I know tonight."

He wrestled with the unfamiliar sense of being backed

into a corner. He wanted to claw his way out but he didn't have enough information to fight with. Did she really know something or was this a fishing expedition for her? Cooper needed to find out what Serena knew. It required him to retreat, which was the most difficult thing to do in the middle of battle.

"I will meet you at the restaurant here at eight," he said as he reluctantly took a step back. "If you run I will hunt you down."

"Why would I run when I have everything I want?" she asked as he turned away.

Cooper kept walking as her earthy laugh rang in his ears. He only had a few hours to find out everything about how Aaron Brock had destroyed Serena Dominguez's life. Dread seeped in his bones as he forced his legs to move. He knew, without a shadow of a doubt, that his father had shown no mercy.

Serena watched Cooper Brock storm off, a dark and menacing figure surrounded by color and light. She slowly exhaled, her breath stuttering past her lips. The ice in her drink rattled and she gripped the glass tighter, refusing to give in to the case of nerves. Her stomach was still in knots and her skin felt cold. She shivered under the heat of the sun and refrained from rubbing her hands against her arms in case he looked back.

Serena's tension didn't evaporate once Cooper was out of view. If anything, his absence made her anxiety coil tighter around her chest. It would be best if she knew where he was at all times. She didn't like surprises, especially those wrapped in a six-foot-three athletic male body.

She had planned on confronting Cooper but she hadn't expected him so soon. News traveled fast and Cooper Brock worked even faster. He had caught her at a disadvantage but she had done her best to hide it. Her parents had taught her that image was everything and hiding what she really felt had become second nature to her.

Serena knew her image was that of a spoiled socialite. She allowed the media to perpetuate that myth. The world only saw the glittery jewelry, the standoffish sunglasses and the haughty smiles. It wasn't who she was but it was her armor. She'd rather people see that than the fear and vulnerability that constantly rolled through her.

And the next time she met Cooper she wouldn't be half-naked and lying down, Serena decided. She would take charge and wouldn't let him trap her. Corner her. Next time she would meet him at eye level and stand toe to toe. And at the end of their meeting, she would walk away with a proud swagger.

She heard the buzz of her cell phone. Serena reached for it and saw how her hands still trembled. It was a good thing Cooper didn't bother noticing the small details. If he had known that his sudden appearance left her unsettled, he would have ruthlessly used that to his advantage.

"Alô?" She managed a breezy tone as she answered the call.

"Serena?" she heard a man ask. The clipped British accent was nothing like Cooper Brock's Southern drawl. "This is Spencer Chatsfield. I want an update."

She pressed her lips together and swallowed back an irritated sigh. She didn't appreciate Spencer checking up on her. He had seemed completely on board when she had presented him with this business opportunity but it felt as if he was having second thoughts. She had everything under control but she knew Spencer had a lot of money riding on this venture.

"It's all going as planned," she announced with supreme confidence. "This morning I won the bid for the Alves property with the money you gave me. I have already arranged a meeting with Cooper Brock and this evening I will make him an offer. He will agree and I will transfer the land to Cooper for the Harrington shares you want." She couldn't wait to present this deal to Cooper and see his expression. Watch the confidence drain from his silvery-gray eyes and be replaced with defeat.

"If the transaction was going to be that simple I would have done it myself. What if he refuses?"

She fully expected Cooper to refuse...at first. "He won't because I have something he wants more," she said with a sly smile. He wanted this more than the land. More than shares to The Harrington.

"He's a Brock. Making deals is in his blood. He never loses."

Serena took a healthy sip of her cocktail as she gathered the last of her patience. Cooper never lost because he had the Brock name backing him up. He didn't know what it was like to make a deal in a position of fear, worried that he would lose everything in an instant. But she was going to change all that. She was going to reclaim her power by stripping him of his own.

"Spencer, we discussed this when I visited you in London," she answered sweetly. Her feminine charm had distracted him then. It was her most successful technique to get what she wanted in the boardroom. "If you didn't think I could negotiate with Cooper Brock, then you shouldn't have fronted me the money."

"If it all goes to plan, Brock gets his deal and I get the shares to The Harrington," Spencer said. "What do you get? Why are you doing this?"

She knew what he was really asking. *What am I missing?* Apparently he no longer believed her explanation when she first proposed this idea. The reason she had given was admittedly weak, but she had couched her answer with the flirtatious smiles and body language that left men flummoxed. She wasn't going to tell him the truth now no matter how much money he had invested in her plan. There was a lot he didn't know and she was going to keep it that way.

"I hope this will show you my abilities for future projects," she lied. "Anyone can gather information but no one can make the intuitive leaps and connections like me."

"Serena," he said in harsh tone, "if you don't get the shares for The Harrington..."

"I have researched Cooper Brock for years," she sharply reminded Spencer. "One could say I'm an expert on him and his father. You will get those shares by the end of the week." She ended the call with an angry stab of her fingertip and tossed the phone onto the stack of business magazines lying next to her on the sand.

Serena lowered her sunglasses onto the bridge of her nose and determinedly stared at the crashing waves. The offensive attack on Cooper Brock was a new feeling for her. She didn't like it because as much as she could predict the outcome, she was still putting herself at risk. Every action, every plan she made up to now, was defensive, protecting what she had.

She breathed in deep, her chest still tight as she inhaled the briny scent of the ocean. She knew what she was doing. Her strategy was solid. Indestructible. She wasn't going to let anything—or anyone—get in her way.

Anticipation fluttered just under her skin. After years of hard work, sacrifice and planning, she was finally ready to battle Cooper Brock. And by the end of the week, she would be the ultimate victor and get her revenge.

CHAPTER TWO

SERENA'S HEELS CLICKED against the floor as she approached the restaurant, the staccato beat matching the jittery pulse at the base of her throat. She reached the dramatic rounded archway and caught a tantalizing whiff of grilled meat and exotic spices. Glancing inside, she found the stark-white walls and blue tile accents bright and welcoming. Serena noticed most of the tables were occupied and instantly recognized a few famous faces.

She smoothed a hand over her hair, wishing it hadn't taken ages to tame the waves into a sleek ponytail. Her hands had been clumsy earlier when she had fixed her hair and makeup. She didn't know why she was so nervous. Everything was going as planned. She was in full armor now from her pink halter dress to her strappy stiletto heels.

She glanced down at the diamond bracelet encircling her wrist and paused. Memories crowded and overlapped in her mind. Some good, some bad. She remembered the day when her father had given the bracelet to her mother.

It had not been a special occasion. Her father never felt the need to wait for a celebration. He enjoyed presenting lavish gifts to her mother for no reason at all. She once thought these extravagant presents represented undying love. It was only when she was older that she'd realized there had been undercurrents of control and reward.

Serena remembered the surprise and pleasure in her mother's glamorous face when she had opened the flat square box from her favorite jeweler's. Serena also recalled the pride that shimmered from her father. The memory was so clear even after all these years because it was one of the last times she had seen those expressions from her parents.

Serena stood very still as she continued to stare at the bracelet. She remembered the defeat in her mother's eyes when she had to sell the jewels after Felipe Dominguez's business crumbled. At the time, Serena had silently sworn that one day she would have the money to buy back every piece of jewelry and return it to her mother.

It had taken her years and she had been so proud when she had hunted down this bracelet and bought it. She had taken it as a sign that their luck was changing for the better. Serena had presented it to her mother, promising to find the other jewels she had surrendered.

But her mother didn't want them. In fact, Beatriz Dominguez had recoiled at the sight of the bracelet. The jewelry—and the memories that accompanied them—was tainted. The bracelet had represented a happier time, when the marriage between Felipe and Beatriz was solid and the family fortune was secure.

Serena rolled the bracelet around her wrist, accepting the sharp edges digging into her palm as she forced down the bitterness. Her mother may not want the jewels, but it had been important to Serena to keep them. They represented happier moments for her and her family. She had continued to track them down and buy them one piece at a time. She had not stopped in her mission until she had acquired every ring, necklace and hair ornament.

They were the only jewelry she owned. The only pieces she wore.

The bracelet was a talisman for her tonight. It served as a reminder of where she had been, what she had gone through and why she was doing this. It gave her focus to keep on this journey when the rest of her family wanted to forget.

"*Boa noite*, Senhora Dominguez," the maître d' welcomed her, his eyes lighting up with masculine pleasure. "Your guest is waiting for you at the bar."

She hesitated, fiercely gripping her evening purse as the surprise rippled through her. Cooper Brock was already here? Before her? She had assumed he would be like most businessmen and arrive late in a failed attempt to set the tone of the evening. The fact that she hadn't anticipated this maneuver sent a wisp of unease down her spine.

"*Obrigada*," she replied softly as she turned to the bar where the older man gestured. It was her custom to arrive first and take early control of the battlefield. Cooper had taken her move. Why? The man relied on his family name and his charm to make things happen. Either he was eager to get this over with or he found her a worthy opponent.

She immediately saw Cooper. He was leaning against the carved wooden bar as if he didn't have a care in the world. His light gray suit and white shirt opened at the neck accented his lean build. She took a moment to study her quarry as he stared at the drink in his hand.

Cooper Brock made her think of the mythical cowboys from the Wild West. She wasn't sure why. Serena had never seen him wear a Stetson over his expensively tousled sandy-blond hair. But she knew he was a man who followed his own code of honor and would risk everything to protect his territory, his family and his woman. He may be the heir to an empire but Cooper created and controlled his own destiny.

She always thought that his craggy face matched his

stubborn personality. It was all angles from his high
cheekbones to the blade of his nose and the slash of his
mouth. But it was his silver eyes that dominated his face.
They were surprisingly expressive, at one moment play-
ful and fierce the next.

Cooper glanced up sharply and her gaze clashed with
his. Her heart leaped violently. She wanted to inhale
deeply but the breath stole from her lungs. She was mesmerized as his features sharpened while he hunched his
shoulders.

This time his eyes flashed with an unspoken challenge
and she darted her gaze away. Her instincts screamed to
keep him in her sight in case he pounced but she ignored
it. Serena steadfastly refused to look at Cooper in the eye
as she walked toward him, keenly aware of the sway of her
hips and the way her silk dress grazed her bare legs. Her
skin prickled as she felt his gaze drift along her curves.
She wondered if the halter dress had been a poor choice.

When she had been getting ready for dinner there had
been a moment when she considered covering herself
from shoulder to knee. She had immediately discarded
the idea. There was no need to hide or change her style.
This dress was part of her armor, her carefully controlled
image. She would not allow Cooper Brock to determine
what she wore.

But as his attention rested on her full breasts, her nipples stinging as they tightened, Serena recalled why she
had hesitated. She was used to men staring at her, wanting her. She often used their reactions to her advantage.
She couldn't do that with Cooper. She instinctively knew
that if she taunted him, the power struggle between them
would shift. The sensual mood she'd create would boomer-
ang back and the desire she felt would be used against her.

Cooper Brock was definitely not a man to tease. The

lust he had for her was barely restrained and it would not take much to unleash it. Just the thought of it made her skin heat and created a pulsating ache low in her belly. This reaction of hers was inconvenient. Distracting. *Wrong.*

"Serena," Cooper said by way of greeting before he motioned for the bartender.

She requested a glass of wine and didn't look in Cooper's direction until it was necessary. "You're here early," she commented lightly, hoping it didn't sound like a complaint. "You must be staying nearby."

"I booked myself here in The Harrington."

Her stomach gave a vicious twist. *That close.* She wasn't sure how she felt about him being under the same terracotta tile roof. She wouldn't be able to get away from him. A man like Cooper Brock couldn't be contained by the bright white walls and iron grille windows. But Serena showed no reaction and waited for her drink under his intense gaze.

Cooper slugged back the rest of his drink. He grimaced from the bite of the hard liquor and set the crystal tumbler down with a thud. "Okay, Serena," he said. "What do you want in exchange for the Alves land?"

She chuckled as she accepted the glass of wine from the bartender. "You Americans. So abrupt and aggressive," she chided. "Do you realize that this is why I was able to swoop in and get the deal?"

Cooper scowled at her. "I don't believe in wasting time."

"You need to relax and socialize." She turned, resting her elbows against the bar as she tilted her head back to meet his silvery-gray eyes. "Learn something about the person with whom you are negotiating. Having a grasp of their native language would be nice."

"I make deals around the world. It would be inefficient—not to mention impossible—to learn all the languages."

"Then don't be surprised if I manage to swoop in and interfere with your deals again and again." How many deals would she have to steal before he struggled with the same uncertainty she'd wrestled with every day for the past decade? It would never be enough. He would never know what it was like to have his security stolen from him, to be paralyzed with fear.

"I won't let that happen." His voice was rough with impatience. "Now, what do you want from me?"

"I am willing to give you the land," she said. She had no use for the Alves property but he didn't need to know that.

He tipped his head back and watched her closely. She knew his mind was whirring as he tried to determine the trap she was laying. "How much are you inflating the price?"

"I'm not." She had toyed with the idea of making a profit from the exchange. Serena equated money with security and the more money she acquired, the more protection she had against the injustices of the world. She knew she could make money from the transaction but it was more important to focus on her main goal. "I will give you the land for the same amount that I paid."

His eyes narrowed as he gave her a dark look of suspicion. "Why would you do that?"

"Because I want something more than money." She took a sip of her wine and the fruity notes burst against her tongue. "I want the shares to The Harrington."

His startled bark of laughter shattered the quiet atmosphere of the bar. "Hell, no."

"Then I guess we have nothing to talk about." She set down her wineglass, picked up her small purse and moved to leave.

He wrapped his hand around her wrist and stopped her. Her limbs went rigid as the wild energy coursed through her body from his simple touch. Serena stared at his dark and calloused hand that covered her diamond bracelet. The anger of seeing a Brock touching her mother's jewelry warred with the traitorous need to yield to his hold.

"Why are you leaving?" Cooper's voice was soft and husky. Almost intimate. "We've only started to negotiate."

"I'm not here to barter," she said coldly. She wasn't going to fall for his charm. "I told you my price."

"Why would I give up those shares?" he asked with a hint of incredulity. "Don't you read the news?"

"Of course." If Cooper had learned anything about her, he would know that her daily routine was consumed by gathering news and information. It was how she gained and protected her wealth.

"This is the worst time to sell or trade my shares. There's a feud raging between the Chatsfields and the Harringtons," Cooper reminded her. "The publicity has increased the bookings at The Harrington, increasing its value."

She yanked out of his grasp but her skin still tingled from his touch. "Why else do you think I want it?"

"That's what I'm trying to figure out." He lowered his head, moving closer. She fought the urge to take a step back. "You apparently know my portfolio and you want something of lesser value? It doesn't make sense."

She thrust out her chin. "Perhaps I have sentimental reasons for wanting the shares."

"A lovers' weekend?" he said in a growl.

She raised an eyebrow. She did not like the possessive quality of his tone. "I'm not one of those women who gets sentimental about sex."

"Good to know." His eyes suddenly sparkled. Serena

didn't know if he was enjoying the thrust and parry of their conversation or if he was imagining a no-strings sexual escapade with her.

"This meeting is not an exploratory conversation," she said in her haughtiest tone. "It's not a discussion and it's not the foundation for negotiations. I am telling you what I want in exchange for the Alves land."

"Then this conversation is over. I am not giving up my shares." Cooper thrust his hands in his pockets and gave a sharp nod to his head. "A pleasure as always, Serena."

She waited until he began to stroll away. "I'm assuming you spoke to your father this afternoon," she said.

Cooper paused and looked over his shoulder. His gray eyes were guarded but he showed no expression. "Of course."

"Does he remember the name Felipe Dominguez?" Her chest tightened as she waited for the answer.

"Yes."

"Hmm," she said, hating how the sound seemed almost strangled. She had often wondered if Aaron Brock would remember the Dominguez name. It had been fourteen years and while his actions had changed the course of their lives, it had meant nothing to him. "What did he say?"

He walked back to the bar and leaned his arm on the smooth wooden counter. "I wouldn't repeat it in front of a lady."

Serena was tempted to roll her eyes. Why would Cooper think she had delicate sensibilities? She had gained quite a vocabulary during her time living in a seedy neighborhood but it wasn't nearly as colorful as the language she heard in the financial industry. "And what excuse did he give for his actions?"

The corner of his mouth pulled in a wry, lopsided smile. "My father is not one to give excuses."

"I'm not surprised," she murmured.

"He said he had teamed up with Felipe Dominguez while negotiating a deal in Rio de Janeiro. But that Dominguez had tried to double-cross him." She saw the cold glint of anger in Cooper's eyes. "My father retaliated."

It was the bare facts, Serena noticed. Did Cooper know the incredible stress Felipe had been under while working with Brock? Felipe was no match for that bully. Her loving father had gradually become cruel and distant. Serena still longed for the man he used to be.

Cooper's summary of the events also failed to include the slow decline of her family's fortune or the devastation they had suffered. "Aaron Brock destroyed everything that belonged to my father."

"My father was protecting what was his," Cooper argued.

"And not caring that a mother and child were collateral damage," she pointed out. The fury, as familiar as a childhood companion, began to swirl inside her. Her mother had suffered more than she had. Beatriz Dominguez had been a vivacious woman but Serena didn't understand her mother's fragility until after her parents' bitter divorce. Too focused on her own loss, Serena hadn't seen the signs until her mother had a breakdown. Beatriz had never been the same. At times it felt that Serena had switched the mother and daughter roles with Beatriz. She was the minder and the protector and she always felt responsible for not taking better care of Beatriz when it mattered the most.

"What was your father's side of the story?" Cooper asked. "Did Dominguez betray my father?"

Serena blinked. She hadn't expected Cooper to ask

those questions. She assumed he would show blind loy-
alty to his family. "Would you believe what I have to say?"

"You were there when it happened," Cooper responded.
"What did you see? What did your father tell you?"

Her father had told her nothing. Absolutely nothing.
Everything she knew had been based on what she had
witnessed and researched. The man who was supposed to
protect and provide for her was unable to stand up to Aaron
Brock. It was harder for her to admit he had retaliated in a
cowardly manner than the fact that he had failed. "I don't
have to rely on my father's words to understand the facts."

Cooper frowned. "Did your father explain anything
to you?"

She wished he had. Everyone had hid the truth from
her despite her constant questions. Had one more person
told her not to worry her pretty little head, she would not
have been held accountable for her actions. "My parents
are traditional," she explained. "They would never share
financial details with anyone, let alone their only child."

"They were trying to protect you."

Did they? She wondered about that. Or were they trying to hide their failures, their shame? She hadn't felt protected. She had felt powerless and set adrift when they
suddenly lost their home with no explanation. Confused
when their status and their closest friends fell away. She
had been scared when the tension and the fights escalated
between her parents. The breakdown of their marriage
had run parallel to the destruction of their fortunes. And
then her mother's emotional stability declined sharply.
Serena had to become the protector of the family when
she didn't know how.

She would never allow herself to feel that powerless
or confused again. She no longer relied on others to take
care of her. It had been the only way she had survived.

"I'm sure your parents discussed business over the dinner table every night."

"I'm sure they did," Cooper drawled. "My parents are obsessed with business."

She frowned. "But they didn't discuss it with you?" He had been the heir. She imagined he had been trained for the role as early as possible.

His eyes were wintry. "What are you trying to ask?"

This was it. Now was the time to use the weapons she had spent what felt like a lifetime gathering. "Do you know what kind of businessman your father is?" she asked, her heart pounding hard against her chest. "What do you know about Aaron Brock?"

Cooper considered his next words. He had done a basic investigation on Serena Dominguez and had learned she was more than a financial genius. The woman was wily and tenacious. She managed to uncover information about companies that legal teams had spent millions to hide. What did she know about the Brock empire?

"My father could be a powerful ally or a dangerous enemy."

"The man was a ruthless bully." She grounded out the last word. "Look at what he did to my father. Aaron put so much pressure on him to be perfect. My father was in constant fear of failing, of disappointing Aaron."

Cooper knew what Felipe had suffered but he wasn't going to sympathize with the man. Cooper had to be perfect and extraordinary in everything he did or he suffered the consequences. But he didn't react like Felipe. Cooper had more to lose and yet he had found the strength to hold on to his principles. "Felipe tried to double-cross my father but got burned."

Serena gave a sharp, angry nod. "My father was once

a businessman who only needed a handshake to do business. That changed when he started working with your father. Aaron Brock allowed no room for weakness or failure. He tore my father down, piece by piece, until he was just a shell of the man he used to be."

That had been Aaron's method throughout Cooper's childhood, too, but Cooper had refused to complain or give up. He had been driven to prove he was worthy of his father's hopes. And he had done things he regretted in the pursuit of gaining Aaron's respect and affection. It took him a long time to realize that nothing he accomplished would make him lovable and worthy to his parents.

But he was their son and heir and he would protect the family empire. He could not allow anything to taint their reputation. Any rumor about his father's business practices would be a failure.

"Felipe was as pure as snow, was he?" He dipped his head until his face was almost touching hers. He refused to let her faint perfume distract him. He wouldn't think about how he was just a kiss away from her mouth. "Check your facts, sweetheart," Cooper said gruffly. "You forget that he betrayed his business partner."

"My father was a victim, but I never suggested he was innocent." Serena's golden eyes glittered with knowing. "I mean, we all have skeletons in our closets, Mr. Brock. I just happen to know every last one of yours."

He pulled back before he could stop himself. It wasn't an act of guilt but Serena's smile was triumphant as if she had hit her target. Did she know everything? His instincts said no. Only he and John Harrington, Jr., knew about his most shameful secret.

"What are you accusing me of?" he asked in an angry hiss. "Go back and look at every deal I've made. I have nothing to hide." Except for one but he had learned his lesson. Sure, some of his deals skirted along the edge of the law, but he had snatched himself back.

She pointed an accusing finger at him. "You know what Aaron did to build his empire and you kept quiet."

"This is what I know—my father had nothing and made something of himself through blood, sweat and tears."

"That's the legend, but you and I know that's not true." She poked her finger against his chest. "Your father built his business by extortion, blackmail and corruption. And I can prove it."

CHAPTER THREE

IMPOSSIBLE. THE WORD reverberated in his head. There was no way that Serena knew about his father's transgressions. Aaron Brock would never have left behind damning evidence. Serena Dominguez had to be bluffing.

Cooper was tempted to close his hand around her finger pressing against his chest. He wanted to step closer so her finger would curve and rest against his breastbone. Prove to Serena that she was no match for him and force her to drop her hand.

The maître d' hesitantly approached them to let them know their table was ready. Cooper closed his eyes and reined in his anger. As much as he resented the intrusion, he needed it. Serena was baiting him as if she had predicted his primitive response.

As they silently followed the man to the restaurant, Cooper automatically reached out to guide Serena, splaying his hand on her back. His fingers accidentally stroked against her bare skin. Cooper's breath hitched in his throat as desire slammed against him. He felt Serena's tension soar before she pulled away and walked ahead of him.

The restaurant was a blur of blue and white as his troubled thoughts clouded his senses. If anyone had greeted him, he wouldn't know. His mind was churning as he ruthlessly pulled back the need to fight. Roar. Defend his territory and his family name in the most elemental way.

He waited until they were alone and seated at the table before he spoke. "I'm calling your bluff, Serena," he said in a low tone as he ruthlessly controlled his temper. "If you had any damaging information, you would have publicized it."

"And how would I have benefited from that?" she asked in an absent murmur. Serena didn't look at him as she studied the oversize menu. "How do you feel about caviar?"

"Serena," he warned.

She glanced up from the menu. "There is a reason why I'm successful in the financial world. Anyone can find information if they're willing to keep digging for it. It's how you use that information to your advantage that matters."

"True," Cooper said. "How you use unsubstantiated rumors matters, as well. Try to act as if these stories are true and it will backfire on you."

She smiled as if his prediction was nothing more than a fanciful idea. "How much do you know about your father's dealings?"

Did she really think he was going to give a direct answer? This socialite might be used to getting everything she asked for but he wasn't going to indulge her. "I've worked in the family business for over ten years."

Serena set down the menu and rested her arms on the smooth white tablecloth. "That's not what I asked. I know of four instances when your father willfully broke the law to crush another company."

A chill swept through him and he struggled not to react. Serena was correct. How had she found out? No one but him and his father knew the details. Cooper was privy to three of those deals because he had been working for his father during that time.

Those were the rare circumstances when Aaron Brock had almost lost a fortune but managed to snap the power from the jaws of destruction. He knew his father wasn't proud of those moments or of his actions. Not that Cooper would admit that to Serena. Nor would his father's conflicted emotions matter to her.

But it meant something to him. Cooper knew his father was driven and goal-oriented. Strong-willed and decisive. Those were the traits they shared, the qualities Aaron Brock developed in him as he taught his only son everything he knew.

Cooper still remembered the sickening feeling that permeated through him when his father had shared those secret details with him as a cautionary tale. He had been appalled by his father's choices. Disturbed that his flesh and blood would be that merciless. And he wondered if time and circumstances would prove that he had inherited those traits.

Cooper didn't agree with his father's methods and refused to follow his lead. It had been a point of contention between them for years. He wasn't close with his parents, yet he was a dutiful son. But would he break the law to save them? He didn't know the answer and that concerned him. How far would he go to protect the family?

Or was it to protect the family business? Cooper gritted his teeth as he realized where his train of thought was turning. The Brock family and the Brock business were so entwined that he couldn't separate the two.

All he knew was that it was his responsibility to protect his family. Even when his father's sins had come back to haunt them. Cooper needed to take any threat seriously. If that meant protecting the Brock name and the business, he would do it.

"Tell me about one of these instances," he encouraged Serena. "This should be entertaining."

"Which one should I mention?" Serena glanced out of the window that overlooked the beach and tapped her finger against her lips. "I know. The deal that happened in Hong Kong. In fact, you were there," she said with nonchalance. He knew she couldn't determine just how much he had been involved with the outcome of that deal. "It had been your first time in charge of negotiations for your family's company and you weren't even out of university."

Cooper remembered. He had believed the people he had been negotiating with were honest. He had almost lost the deal that could have weakened the family's business. It was the first time he had seen just how hard and ruthless his father could be. It was also the last time he had disappointed his father.

"Did you know that Aaron saved the deal by using extortion and intimidation?"

He had found that out later. The guilt and responsibility had weighed on him. He had been so far out of his depth that it required his father to do whatever was necessary to protect him and the business.

That moment of realization was also when he knew he would not make the same choices as his father. He would build the Brock empire to be invincible but he would do it his way. He would prove to his father that he was just as powerful. That he was smarter, stronger and better. That he would never get into that kind of trouble where he had to make those choices.

"I guess that is how your parents protected you," she said.

Cooper's mouth twisted. He used to think that. That Aaron Brock would do anything to protect him. But his father stamped out that naive thought very quickly. Aaron had to demonstrate power and so did his son.

"I remember Hong Kong very differently," he finally said. "I'm interested in seeing this proof of yours."

"Do you think I walk around with it on my laptop? Or keep it in the hotel safe? No, I have all of the physical proof far away from here."

Physical? Did that mean she had found original documents and firsthand accounts? Dread pulled at him in all directions. This was worse than he imagined. "How long have you been gathering these stories?"

"They are not stories," she insisted. "They are facts."

"How long?" he repeated.

"Years." She shrugged as if her answer didn't matter. "It has been a hobby of mine since I was a teenager."

Hobby? An obsession, more like it. Most debutantes filled their days with shopping and parties, not systematically gathering condemning evidence on a powerful company. Why would she spend so much time on something when she couldn't change the outcome? What kind of socialite was she?

When Serena thrust her chin out with defiance he wondered if she saw the questions in his eyes. "However," she said, "I'm willing to keep quiet about what I have found in exchange for the Harrington shares."

"I don't believe you."

"That I have proof?" she said with a scowl. "Or that I won't use it?"

All of it, Cooper decided. It wasn't adding up. Why would someone spend years gathering information on the person she accused of ruining her life and then promise she wouldn't use it? The Harrington shares were worth a lot, but were they enough to abandon her lifelong pursuit for revenge?

He could not give up the shares. He needed them for his own protection. Cooper might have a stellar reputation in the business world but no one knew about his first solo business deal with John Harrington, Jr.

Cooper was still ashamed of how he had obtained his first deal. He had been desperate to prove himself and show that he didn't need his father's name or influence to be a success. John Jr. knew how hungry Cooper was for negotiating a deal and had dangled insider knowledge in front of him. Cooper grabbed at it like a starving man. His first deal was huge and he made a stunning debut in the financial world. It helped him create a legendary image but only John Jr. knew the truth.

It was only a matter of time before John Harrington, Jr., used that information and the truth could destroy Cooper. When he had won the shares Harrington couldn't afford to gamble away, Cooper knew he could keep John quiet. The Harrington shares were Cooper's insurance for now.

"I want to see this so-called proof before I even consider giving up the shares," he told Serena.

She glared at him. "I just gave it to you. I didn't make it up. How would I have known the places and people unless I had the facts?"

"You repeated hearsay and rumors," Cooper declared. "I won't allow myself to be blackmailed for something that doesn't exist."

Her fingers bunched into a fist. She was obviously offended that he questioned her word and the work she had put so much effort into. "As I told you," she bit out, "I don't have the papers with me."

Cooper nodded as if he was placating a child about to have a temper tantrum. "Of course you don't."

"And it would take too long to have them sent here," she almost growled.

Cooper tilted his head. *Too long?* "Are we on a deadline?"

"Yes." She pressed her lips together. He could see how she gathered her courage before she made her ultimatum. "If you don't agree with this deal by the end of the week, then I will release the information about your father to the press."

Hell. He could not let that happen. He needed to get her to see reason and gain her sympathy before she made a move. That required him to change tactics.

"Serena, I'm sure we can come up with an agreement that will satisfy both of us." He covered her hand with his. His thumb grazed her wrist and he felt the kick of her pulse. He glanced up, startled, and saw the interest widening her eyes as the pleasure chased across her face. She snatched her hand away as if she'd been bit by something dangerous.

Serena Dominguez had been very careful around him. She had shut down his propositions and invitations. His flirtatious banter had been met with cool disdain. But she couldn't hide her body's reaction. She could no longer conceal the way her lips parted or the flush in her cheeks. She didn't seem aware of her body language when she battled with him. Serena would often get closer, open and inviting, as if she forgot all the reasons she needed to maintain a distance.

"You can't sweet-talk me into changing my mind," she warned.

He bet he could. His smile was slow and lazy. Confident as the thrill of the hunt sizzled through his chest. As much as she tried to fight it, Serena Dominguez was attracted to him. He had just discovered her weakness.

Unfortunately, the attraction they shared was his weakness, too. He hadn't seen that she was a worthy opponent until it was too late. But he knew he could use it to his benefit. He could get close to the fire without getting scorched. And, if he played this right, he would get Serena in his bed and on his side.

Serena didn't like his seductive smile. She didn't like how it sparked an uncontrollable excitement in her. The hum of energy danced in her veins and she needed it to stop. She placed her hands in her lap and absently stroked her wrist as if it had been burned.

How did Cooper have this kind of power over her? One grazing touch and she couldn't think about anything else. It didn't make sense. He had the Brock blood running through his veins. She should be shuddering with revulsion at the thought of breaking bread with him.

No man had power over her. Financially. Physically. Emotionally. She had witnessed how her mother's future had been decided on by her father's whims and choices. Serena didn't understand why any woman would surrender that kind of control over their lives.

Cooper leaned forward and she automatically pressed her spine against the ornate wood chair. "Is this why you have avoided me all month?" he asked in a husky voice. "Because you see me as the enemy?"

"How could I avoid you?" she asked irritably. "You were everywhere I turned."

"You refused every invitation I offered."

"You mean every indecent proposal," she snapped. He had been direct but never crude or coarse. She sensed the savage hunger beneath his veneer of civility, yet the man managed to make the promise of a one-night stand sound like a sacred experience. She rejected him outright but he didn't give up. If anything, his invitations became more extravagant and imaginative. It had become a game between them.

There were moments when she wished she could have entertained the idea. A few times she wanted to forget about this revenge. Just for one night. Break free from the dark emotions that suffocated her. Explore the attraction she shared with Cooper. Enjoy life.

That was when she knew Cooper Brock was very dangerous. Not once had she considered stepping back from her vengeful plans until she met him. It worried her. She didn't know why she felt that way. Did it mean her drive was weakening? Or that her desire for Cooper was stronger?

He propped his elbow on the table and rested his strong chin against his hand. "Why didn't you say yes?"

Serena frowned. The man's arrogance was reaching legendary proportions. "I wasn't interested."

"Yes, you were. From the moment we saw each other."

She fell into silence as she remembered the first time she had seen Cooper. It was one of the few moments in her life when she'd followed an impulse and didn't consider the risks. She had regretted it ever since.

Serena had been in London and heard Cooper was going to be the guest speaker at a charity dinner. She had decided to attend so she could study him from afar. It hadn't quite worked out that way. He had noticed her the moment she had stepped into the ballroom.

"Why were you there that night?" Cooper asked, and his mouth tilted into a lopsided grin. "Was it to meet me? You had been so fascinated with what you had already learned that you needed to see me in the flesh?"

Cooper's teasing comment wasn't that far off from the truth. She had been reluctantly impressed by his achievements and she'd believed—hoped—he wouldn't live up to the hype. As much as she tried to convince herself that he got where he was because of his name, she had a feeling he would have been a success no matter what.

"I wanted to support a worthy cause," she said primly. Serena didn't feel the need to encourage his oversize ego.

"Really?" His Southern drawl was thick and sexy. "What was the charity for?"

Her mind went blank. Serena's eyes widened as she tried to recall the charity's logo but it was all a little fuzzy. Her full attention had been on Cooper Brock. From the amused gleam in his eyes, Cooper knew it.

"It was one of the many events I've attended in the past month. They all blend together," she argued. "What do you remember from that night?"

"Your hair was pulled back in a severe knot," he said quietly as his features softened, "and you wore a navy blue dress."

She gave a jerk of surprise. "How— *Why* do you remember that?" And why did she remember every detail about him that night from the way his designer suit hung from his shoulders to the stubble shadowing his angular jaw?

"I remember that dress was better suited for a nun." He shook his head and smiled at her. "Promise me you'll never wear it again. Do mankind a favor and burn it."

Serena pursed her lips, refusing to return his smile. The dress had been dowdy for a reason. She had decided to follow the unofficial dress code of her peers and chose dark, conservative clothes. She had worn no jewelry and a minimum of makeup but it didn't help. She had still stood out. "I was trying to blend in with the other guests."

Her plan had been to stay in the shadows and get lost in the crowd while she studied him. Cooper Brock had been easy to find. Everyone had a tendency to gravitate to him. He had been holding court in the hotel ballroom, surrounded by titans of industries who were hanging on to his every word.

And then he noticed her when she crossed the threshold. He had done a double take and his voice had trailed off. Cooper had reared his head back as if he had been struck. And the moment their eyes met…

Their gazes held as she remembered that moment of impact. She knew Cooper was remembering it, too. Serena's skin grew hot and she felt an insistent tug low in her belly. That instantaneous connection had been scary, exciting and shocking. Serena was used to wielding power over men, but not like this. And no man had made her want to capitulate immediately. Completely.

She had been tempted to turn on her heels and run but she also knew it would have been useless. Cooper Brock would have pursued her. And she would have considered letting him catch her. That had knocked some sense into her. Serena had known that her only option was to stand up to him and defy every wish he made.

She wondered how strong his desire was now that he knew she had the power to destroy him. At the moment it was so thick it was almost tangible. But how quickly would it disappear once he realized she was going to go through with her revenge? Would he still watch her silently with that slumberous look when she went back on her word? Would he want to caress her after she told the whole world how his father conducted business?

As much as the attraction between them intrigued her, she wasn't going to submit to it. She was going to toy with Cooper, let him know what it was like to lose everything.

She was going to crush the Brock empire just as they had crushed her father's company.

And then she was going to discard Cooper Brock and move on with her life.

CHAPTER FOUR

SERENA SET DOWN her small coffee cup over an hour later and frowned as she watched Cooper on the other side of the table. "I should be the one paying for the dinner. You are my guest."

"So you said." Cooper didn't look up as he signed the bill. "Repeatedly."

The man seemed to find the idea of a woman paying for his meal deeply offensive. She had found his traditional view entertaining until she realized he was serious. His comments were not designed to irritate her. Cooper Brock truly believed it was a man's duty—a man's right—to provide.

Nothing she said or did could sway him to change his mind and she had grudgingly conceded this skirmish. If she had caused a scene she doubted he would have backed down. She had not met a man who was as stubborn or as certain of his beliefs.

She had discovered over dinner that Cooper Brock had very strong opinions. Trepidation curled around her chest and squeezed hard. If he felt his family had done nothing wrong, would he sign over the shares to prevent the release of the information she had? For the first time since she proposed the idea to Spencer Chatsfield, Serena wasn't so sure. There was a very good chance that this strategy would not work.

It had to work. She didn't want to think of the financial repercussions if it didn't. Serena willed herself not to panic. She waited for this moment because she understood what the Alves land represented to Cooper. It was his ultimate ambition to get the one deal his father could not.

This was the only reason why she stepped out of her safe corner and challenged him. He had not been as emotionally invested in a deal like the Alves land. He took the interference personally. She needed to have more faith in her research and strategy. Now was not the time to have second thoughts.

"Shall we?" he asked as he rose and walked around the table to assist her.

Serena reluctantly accepted his help as she got up from her seat. She had found a perverse joy in having dinner with Cooper. It was like playing chess with a grand master. He had a sharp mind and was a brilliant conversationalist. He could have her laughing one moment and debating vociferously with him the next. She had to think several moves ahead of him and that was unusual for her. Most of the time she was waiting for her dinner companions to catch up with her.

And at some point during the evening Cooper had decided on his negotiating tactic, Serena thought as they left the restaurant, the cool breeze wafting over her skin. He was going to use his sex appeal and raw masculinity to soften her stance. It was a risky move on his part since she had refused him all these weeks.

He was definitely using his charm to gain her sympathy. Did he think that one encounter with him would turn her head? He had great confidence in his skills if he thought she would eventually find it difficult to destroy him.

It wouldn't work, she decided with a grim smile. She knew how to be ruthless. How to hold on to the anger and feed from it to get the job done. It had been the only way to get out of sudden poverty and provide for her family.

Cooper tilted his head back as the breeze ruffled his short blond hair. She found it surprising that a man with such wealth and power, a man who had everything, would find pleasure in something so simple.

"Let's walk along the beach," he suggested.

Have a moonlit stroll? Could he be more obvious? She wanted to roll her eyes but she found herself giving a nod. She was curious to see what his next move would be. Serena slipped off her stiletto heels and walked with Cooper on the pristine beach, staying at least an arm's length away.

The sand was soft and cool against her bare feet. She heard the rhythmic roll of the waves and the breeze tugging at the palm trees. For a moment she remembered one of the many beach getaways she and her family used to take. Those stolen moments had been fun and adventurous, filled with love and laughter.

When was the last time she had taken the time to enjoy the world around her? Serena glanced at Cooper. Or had been alone with a man late at night?

A long time, she admitted to herself as she followed Cooper to the water's edge. Too long. She often told her matchmaking relatives that she didn't have time to date. It took commitment to build a fortune that could protect her and her family. While her friends were getting on with their lives, she had been caught in the past, researching the Brock empire and following every lead so she could take them down.

And once she had readjusted her target to Cooper Brock, she gradually found that no man could compare. It wasn't his achievements that she found fascinating, but rather the way he had handled disappointments and the rare failure. The man didn't have the Midas touch everyone assumed. But his tenacity and intelligence grabbed her attention. She also admired that he did not abuse the power that was always in his firm grasp.

Of course, he never faced the need to break the law, Serena reminded herself. Aaron Brock did the dirty work and Cooper reaped the benefits.

But soon he would know what it felt like to lose everything. To be collateral damage and not have the power to stop it. Suddenly and without warning. He would find out what it was like to be alone and afraid.

It shouldn't matter how Cooper would handle the reversal of fortune. She didn't want to care if or how he would recover. Why was she curious? No one cared how she had survived. No one thought about her. She had been an innocent bystander. Voiceless. Powerless. Meaningless.

But the Brock family would remember her name after this week. Her revenge had been an intense and exhausting journey but it was almost over. Once she dismantled the Brock empire, she could relax and...

Serena frowned when she couldn't complete that thought. And what? She wasn't sure. She hadn't allowed herself to think that far ahead. She didn't know what to do with the rest of her life. What would make her get out of bed each morning? How would she find the happiness that had eluded her? She couldn't remember the last time she had been happy and fulfilled.

"You're very quiet." Cooper was watching the waves as he slid his hands into his pockets. "Are you still plotting my demise?"

The teasing lilt of his voice rankled. Did he find her revenge a lark? Was her lifelong mission humorous to him? "You don't take me very seriously, do you?" Her voice sounded rough to her ears. "That would be a mistake."

He turned away from the ocean and looked at her. He didn't seem surprised by her angry expression. He paused and she knew he was choosing his words carefully. "I believe you have very strong emotions about what happened," Cooper said. "But fourteen years is a long time to hold on to the need for revenge."

It was. Her journey in and out of poverty had not defined her as much as her drive to destroy the Brock empire. She didn't give up or accept her circumstances. It had lit a fire in her that made her believe she could accomplish anything if she worked hard enough.

"You had plenty of opportunities to come forward with this so-called evidence," he said. "Why now? Why not two years ago?"

She wished she had acted two years ago but she hadn't felt ready. She knew she needed more. More information, more power, more courage. She was facing a giant alone. She had no support and no one was watching her back. Her parents were too afraid, too traumatized, to even discuss the idea of vengeance.

"I'm not reckless like you," she finally said, clasping her evening purse and shoes against her. "I made my fortune by being methodical."

"But you are not diabolical," Cooper pointed out.

"You don't know that." For all he knew she could be on her best behavior.

His eyes narrowed as he studied her. "You know what I think?"

She looked away and stared at the crashing waves on

the shadowy beach. "I'm breathless with anticipation to find out."

He took a step closer and her muscles locked. Serena felt as if she was in fight-or-flight mode. She truly didn't know which choice she would make if he reached for her.

"Either you don't have the proof," Cooper said softly, "or you don't have the killer instinct."

Serena turned her head abruptly. Why was he taunting her? Did he think she would unsheathe her claws the moment he questioned her determination? She had more control than that. "And you make this assumption on what? The fact that I'm a woman?"

"Not at all. I've known women who could be dangerous and vengeful."

She was sure every one of them had been an ex-lover.

"But the revenge you're seeking is obsolete," he continued gently. "It no longer applies."

Obsolete? Her knees almost buckled as the rage, hot and bitter, poured through her.

"You directed your misplaced anger onto my father, but he had retired before you decided to act."

Serena's arms and legs shook as the dark fury whipped through her. "Misplaced?" Her voice cracked.

"Now you direct this anger onto me and it doesn't make sense," Cooper continued as if she hadn't spoken. "I have done nothing to your family."

"You benefited from the crimes your father committed," she said, her voice lashing with anger. "You lived in luxury that you didn't deserve and were given so many opportunities you didn't earn. You never questioned that you could afford the best education and you waltzed fearlessly through life knowing that your future was bright. That should have been my path but your father stole it from me."

Cooper shook his head. "You are wrong. Your father stole it from you."

Serena inhaled sharply. "How dare you."

"He stole your security and your future when he chose to betray his business partner." Cooper stretched his arms out. "He's the one you should be angry at."

She would not listen to this. She would not allow Cooper to poison her mind. There had been a time when she had been furious at her father. She had wondered why he felt he had the power, the right, to betray Aaron Brock. Why couldn't he have walked away? Why couldn't he have been strong enough to stand up to Aaron and hold on to his beliefs?

But she had kept that to herself. Her father had been fragile, suffering with the guilt and shame. If Felipe Dominguez knew how she viewed him, it would have been the final blow.

"What Aaron did was excessive," she argued. "He didn't just retaliate. He demolished everything my father had. The punishment did not fit the crime."

Cooper looked away, the lines that bracketed his mouth deepening. "Then why isn't your father fighting back?"

"Because he can't," she said in a low growl.

"Why did he send his daughter into battle?" His mouth twisted with distaste. "What kind of man hides behind a woman?"

She gripped her shoes as she controlled the urge to throw them at Cooper's head. "Say what you will about me but you do not talk about my father that way."

Cooper watched her as if she was a curiosity. "He's a grown man. He doesn't need your protection."

"Yes, he does!" Serena blurted out the words and immediately regretted it. She didn't want anyone—least of all a Brock—to know how weak and defenseless her parents were.

"He doesn't need you to fight his battles."

"My father has a different set of skills," she argued, thinking fast. She needed to emphasize Felipe's strengths. Image was everything. "That's why your father joined forces with him in the first place. My father is debonair and the life of the party. He can make anyone feel special."

"I understand he retired years ago."

"Retired?" She drew her head back. "Where did you hear that? Your research team needs to be fired on the spot. My father is always working on a deal." Although none of them seemed to gain traction. Felipe Dominguez still refused to believe that no one wanted to invest in him.

"But you support him financially," Cooper said.

Serena thrust her chin out. She knew all about his belief that a man should be the provider but she would not let him diminish her father. "There is nothing wrong with providing for my family."

"And who looks after you?"

No one. And even if someone tried, she wouldn't know how to accept that help. She wouldn't trust it, always wondering when the support would be yanked away. From her experience, any assistance disappeared when she needed it the most. When she had asked and begged for it. She would not put herself in that position again. "I can take care of myself. I've had to ever since Aaron destroyed my world."

"He did not ruin your family. From the sounds of it, Felipe would have self-destructed eventually. My father only sped up the process."

Serena wanted to snarl at him. "You don't know what you're talking about."

"You didn't describe your father as a good businessman," he pointed out. "You said he was debonair and the life of the party. It was all window dressing. He's like a chameleon and adapted to please whoever was in power. He didn't have the courage to face opposition."

"My father didn't do anything illegal," she told Cooper, the stiletto heels digging into her palms.

"True," he admitted, "but his ethics and moral standards were definitely questionable. His business was going to fall down like a house of cards and he didn't want to believe it, always thinking the next deal was going to pull him through. I'm surprised my father didn't know. I guess he had fallen for Felipe's smoke and mirrors."

Serena was surprised that Cooper understood what kind of man her father was. Felipe had the soul of a gambler and believed luck was always around the corner, even after they had lost everything. All Felipe needed to do was maintain his suave image and convince others that he was successful. Once Serena had realized this about her father, she knew she could no longer rely on him. She had felt as if her childhood, her innocence, had been stripped the moment she could no longer trust Felipe would take care of the family.

Cooper sighed. "And your mother would have eventually left Felipe for a richer man."

She flinched. "My mother is not a gold digger." Her mother sought security over love. Serena understood that need but she disagreed with Beatriz's desire to have a strong and successful man to depend upon. Serena believed relying on anyone—especially a man—was the biggest risk a woman could make.

Cooper crossed his arms. "I believe she's living in London," he said nonchalantly. "What is it that she does?"

Her nostrils flared as she held the last shred of her temper. Cooper knew that her mother was a kept woman for a very wealthy, much older gentleman. Once again, Beatriz Dominguez had made the questionable decision to have a man control her finances and her future. This so-called security could be withdrawn at any moment and for no reason at all. She didn't understand her mother's choice but she didn't appreciate Cooper's tone.

"I got it, cowboy." She raised her hands high, her shoes dangling from her fingers as she gestured her defeat. "You think my life would have turned out this way no matter what. Aaron Brock had nothing to do with my father's fall from grace. But you're wrong."

"And I also think you are fixated on something that you can't change."

Serena ignored that. She had heard that plenty of times over the years. No one seemed to understand that if she demonstrated power and weakened the Brocks, even for just a moment, she could prove to herself that she no longer had to fear them. That if she stood up to the family that had created her worst nightmare, she could conquer anything.

"Your parents aren't fighting for what they think is an injustice," Cooper pointed out. "They've moved on. Why haven't you?"

"They were too busy trying to survive to fight back." Serena glanced at the hotel over her shoulder. She wanted to run back to her room. Get away as fast as she could.

"No, that's not it. You hung on to this revenge idea because it's your nature. You have this passion inside you and you don't know where to focus it."

She jerked her head back and stared at Cooper. "You're suddenly an expert on me?"

"I noticed it the moment we met." He strode toward her as if he was done with this conversation. "It's what drew me to you."

"That's ridiculous." She scurried back. "I tried to keep you away from me. I did not encourage you at any time."

"Your passion is something you can't hide," he said as if the words were torn from deep within him. "It radiates from you."

"I believe that's my rage you're seeing."

"You are scared of that passion."

"I am not!" She realized she was shouting. Serena relaxed her grip on her shoes and purse and lowered her voice. "If anyone should be scared of it, it's you."

"Why?" He flashed a lopsided smile. "I welcome it. I want to see more of it."

She watched him with great caution. He seemed to genuinely mean what he said. "Be careful what you wish for."

"You poured all of your focus and energy into revenge because you had nowhere else to direct it," he explained as he reached for her. "It's consumed you for years but it's not enough anymore."

Serena was startled when he wrapped his arm around her waist. "I'm sure you have plenty of ideas on where I should focus my passion," she said.

He dragged her against him. "On me, of course."

"I am focusing it all on you," Serena said through her clenched teeth. She was very aware of how small and delicate she felt against his hard muscular chest.

"I'm honored." Cooper stroked his fingers along her spine. His smile widened when he felt her shiver of pleasure. "But you can't deny the attraction between us."

She growled low in her throat. "Trust a man to make this all about sex."

"I want the passion to wash over me." His voice was low and seductive. "I want to see it reach its full power and then I want to…"

"Tame it?" She tried to break free but his hold tightened. "Dream on. I will never allow you that close to me."

"We would be great together," he murmured as he bent his head. "You know it but you won't consider it. You are giving up something that could be amazing."

Serena knew there was some truth in what he said. She wanted to be with Cooper. Even for just one night but she couldn't allow it. Her plans were holding her back. Her revenge was always preventing her from living to the fullest.

"Your need to retaliate is destroying you," Cooper whispered. "Destroying your life. You have the power to stop it."

She wished she could stop it. Her world had become small and narrow. Numbing. She knew there was something more out there and she ached to find it. She could discover it right now with Cooper.

His mouth pressed against her ear. "Let me show you what it can be like when you just let go."

Let go? Serena gasped. She couldn't. She wanted to but she was afraid to let go. Her vengeance was the only constant thing in her life. What would become of her, what would she turn into, if she didn't have that?

She tried to push away, her shoes and purse bumping ineffectively against his broad shoulders. "Do you usually make a point of sleeping with the enemy?"

"No, but I don't see you as the enemy."

"That is a mistake," she insisted. "You should."

"You don't want to hurt me." He rubbed his hand against her back. "You want to be with me."

"Are you kidding?" She pulled away abruptly and was almost surprised he had let her go. "I am not interested in going to bed with you, Mr. Brock."

He laughed. "Why so formal, Serena? Call me Cooper.

And you want me to take you to bed. I promise you have nothing to be scared about."

She scoffed at his words. "I've seen what a Brock can do."

The amusement died in his eyes. "You're confusing me with my father. Is that why you call me Mr. Brock?"

"And you're confusing me with those lingerie models you date who cling to your every word," she told him. "I cannot be tricked that easily."

"I've wanted you even before I knew what you were after," he reminded her.

"But will you want me after I get the shares?" she asked as she took a few backward steps. "Will you still look at me that way if we don't come to an agreement? If I destroy your business, your future? No, I don't think so."

His expression darkened. "Do you think I can just turn this off?"

It suddenly occurred to her that he didn't want this attraction, this crippling lust, any more than she did. "I think you can," she replied slowly. "And I think you will when this deal doesn't go your way."

"I'm sure we can come up with a compromise," he said. "We can both get everything we need."

What kind of compromise? What was he willing to offer? Her eyes widened. Why was she considering a compromise? That was not enough. She had gone through too much pain and suffering to settle. She wanted to see the defeat in Cooper's eyes.

Cooper had the power to lull her senses even in an argument. This man was very dangerous. She had to make a retreat before she lost any more ground.

She turned away and marched to the hotel. "I've listened to you enough," she said over her shoulder. "You have until tomorrow evening to agree to my terms. If you don't, then I am releasing the information I have on your father."

CHAPTER FIVE

COOPER STRODE THROUGH the luxurious spa, noticing it was almost empty this early in the morning. The white-on-white interior design was probably supposed to be calming, but it did nothing to relax him. Only one thought went through his head: he was not going to be bested by a spoiled princess.

He rounded the corner and passed by a sauna. He knew Serena wouldn't be there. Not enough pampering included in that treatment. Serena Dominguez was a glamorous woman who expected a certain level of comfort. She was avoiding him and what better way to hide than having a full day at a world-renowned spa? She probably thought he wouldn't consider looking for her here.

It was true that Cooper hadn't been in this part of the hotel grounds. If he wanted to get rid of tension, he would run hard on the beach or swim in the ocean to the point of exhaustion. He had already completed a punishing circuit at the health club. It didn't clear his head or tame the anger inside him. He refused to wait around anymore. He had to talk some sense into Serena.

Cooper didn't think it would do much good but it was worth a gamble. He knew all about rich girls who had too much time on their hands and didn't get enough attention. He had dated quite a few until he realized they weren't worth the aggravation. One thing he learned was if you let them have their way, they became very dangerous.

Why did he think Serena would be different? He had tried to be reasonable. He'd even tried to be sympathetic, which was not his strong suit. Cooper thought he had given a solid argument when they had walked along the beach the night before. She needed to let go of this idea of revenge before she wasted her life on something that didn't matter. It wasn't going to make a difference other than soothe her hurt feelings for a moment.

If Serena Dominguez thought she could back him into a corner and blackmail him into surrendering to her will, then she was going to learn that no one screwed with a Brock.

Cooper spotted the closed white door that led to Serena's aromatherapy treatment. He rolled back his shoulders and took in a deep breath. He knew he couldn't come on strong. He couldn't show the anger, the indignation, flowing through him.

If his opponent had been a man, he would be a whirlwind of aggression and power. But his opponent was known as the Brazilian Bombshell among his peers. She was a young woman who used her beauty and femininity to get her way. The only way to fight back was to use his masculine charm.

And if she didn't get her way, she would have one epic tantrum. Cooper clenched his fists as he imagined the aftermath. Serena Dominguez would not only ruin his family and his business, but she would also destroy the lives of his employees and the community the Brock empire supported. They were his responsibilities and he could not live with himself if he let everyone down.

But the spoiled little princess didn't think about those innocent people. Had she considered them or was her tunnel vision too focused on the Brock family? No, it was all about her. About how she didn't get the life she had expected. The lifestyle she thought she deserved.

Cooper flexed his hands and smoothed down his tie before he buttoned his suit jacket. Serena needed to grow up and discover that the world did not revolve around her. And he was going to enjoy teaching her that lesson.

Cooper swung open the door and marched inside the steamy room. He stopped abruptly when he discovered Serena was in a white sunken bath. His sharp reflexes shut down, his senses overwhelmed as his mind registered one thing at a time. The surprise in Serena's eyes. The heavy scent of roses. Her hair pulled up high into a topknot. A blanket of dark red rose petals. Her wet skin. A peek of her dark pink nipples under the clear water.

"Oh, not again!" she said. He couldn't have heard that correctly. What did she mean by again? "Get out."

Wild lust slammed through his body with such force that his knees threatened to buckle. He drew in a breath and the floral scent pierced the fog in his brain. He knew from this moment on he would think of Serena like this when he saw a rose.

"Feeling stressed?" he asked, annoyed at the husky timbre in his voice as he closed the door behind him. "I guess you would. It's not every day that you would try to threaten a billion-dollar corporation. So many things can go wrong. It could backfire on you."

"Did you hear me?" She motioned wildly at the door. "Get out."

Cooper responded silently by leaning against the door and crossing his arms. Let her think it was a power move and not because he needed support.

She slapped her hands against the water. The violent

splash was loud and ineffective. "I will scream this place down."

He watched the rose petals dance along the ripples, offering him another tantalizing peek of her body. This was a mistake. He should leave and yet he couldn't move. "No one's around. They think I'm here for a scandalous rendezvous." It had been surprisingly easy to get the employees out of the way. Money helped, but everyone working at the hotel seemed to think he was carrying on a torrid affair with Serena. "Anyway, I'm simply having a conversation with you."

She glared at him. "You weren't invited here."

He shrugged. As if that had ever stopped him before. He wasn't one to wait for a chair at the table. "If you want me to leave, you will have to remove me from the room yourself."

"You think I won't? You may be taller and stronger than me, but that doesn't mean I can't fight you."

Cooper would never touch a woman in anger and part of him hoped Serena wasn't aware of that. She would use it to her advantage. He also noticed she didn't care about her nudity. This woman was not modest. She used her feminine charms to get her way. Her clothes emphasized her toned body and always offered a flash of cleavage or leg. He wanted to see if she would rise from the bath and press her wet, naked body against his as she wrestled for control.

Damn, he had to focus. He kept his eyes on her bare face. She was still stunning without makeup and her hair gathered in a messy topknot. More approachable, he decided. "We need to talk."

"Here? Now?" She gestured at the water and his attention followed. His gaze caught on the drifting rose petals that revealed her generous hip. "While I'm taking a bath?"

"I don't have a problem with it." His voice sounded gruff and he willed his attention back to her golden eyes. "Do you?"

She leaned back and rested her arms against the edge of the sunken tub. "I will if you try to join me."

"Are you sure?" He imagined shucking off his clothes as Serena watched him with barely contained hunger. The water would be warm and silky as he entered the bath. He would kneel between Serena's legs as she stretched out her arms and invited him closer...

"I don't like to share." Serena's declaration broke his reverie.

"I don't doubt it," he murmured.

Her sigh echoed in the small room. "What is so urgent that you had to track me down this early in the morning?"

"Let's say I don't give you the Harrington shares and you release the documents you supposedly have on my father." He didn't want to sell the shares. Cooper needed to find an alternative. The shares protected him from John Harrington, Jr., but selling them would protect his father. Either course of action would hurt the Brock empire. He couldn't let that happen under his watch. He didn't like that the need to be perfect and successful in the eyes of his parents was still ingrained in him. "What do you think will happen next?"

She gave a smile that reminded him of a cold-blooded reptile. It diminished the vibrant energy he associated with her. He didn't think Serena had the capability of being vicious until this moment.

"Aaron Brock will get hit hard when the news breaks," Serena predicted. "It will weaken him and he'll be thrown into a feeding frenzy where everyone will want to tear a piece off him. The press, the legal system, his enemies."

Cooper knew it would be open season on the Brock family.

"Then," Serena continued as she relished the scenario, "when he doesn't think there's anything left, the people he had once trusted will scavenge his bones."

He had no doubt that would happen. He'd seen how allies turned to enemies when they caught the scent of weakness. "Is that what happened to Felipe?"

Her smile vanished and she looked away. "It happened to all of us. Rumors and whispers have a way of creating roots," she said in a low, faraway voice. "You can chop and hack at them but they never go away. At times, they seem to multiply."

Cooper knew she was trapped in some unpleasant memories. He wasn't going to ask for details. He didn't want to care. She was trying to play on his emotions and his need to protect the vulnerable. He wasn't going to fall for it. He had to focus on protecting the Brock empire. That was all that mattered. It was the only thing his parents wanted from him and he could not fail.

Serena cleared her throat and dipped her hand in the bathwater. She gathered a few of the crimson petals and crushed them in her fist. "Aaron will then lose all that he has accumulated throughout his lifetime."

"No, he won't." His father knew how to protect his wealth. He wouldn't let it all fall into the hands of his enemies.

"He will," she said with certainty as she let the petals fall from her hand. "At first, he will sell the things he doesn't think he truly needs. The things he tells himself that he can always buy back when the ordeal is over."

"It will never get that far." Cooper wouldn't let his parents suffer like that.

She acted as if he hadn't spoken. "And then he will

start selling what is important and sentimental." She absently rubbed one of her gold earrings. "He'll sell part of his heritage. His soul. His hopes and dreams as he tries to survive day to day."

Her voice trailed off and she fell into a troubled silence. "And then what?" he prompted.

"He'll live his remaining days in ruins," she declared as if she was the judge, jury and executioner.

"Not if I have anything to say about it," he said in a harsh tone.

"It would be out of your hands."

"If you release that information, hunting season will be declared on me, not my father." He flattened his hands against his chest. "I'm the one in charge now and I'm the one responsible."

"You inherited Aaron's legacy," she admitted, "but that doesn't mean he will be absolved. His former colleagues and enemies will go after him."

"Most of them are gone or retired." The men were old, worn-out and wanted peace and quiet. Unlike his father. "And while I fight to save the Brock empire, my father will spend every waking moment going after you."

There was a moment of panic that flashed through her eyes. He caught a glimpse of the frightened young woman whose life had crashed around her. Serena's eyelashes fluttered and then it was as if the fear hadn't existed. "Bring it on."

Cooper exhaled sharply. She couldn't be that brave. "You don't mean it. You don't want his wrath—or mine—coming down on you."

Serena sat forward, curling her arms around her bent knees. A few petals rested on her golden-brown skin. "Cooper, do you believe in fighting for justice?"

He thought he did, but his definition of justice was

different from hers. "What you're doing isn't justice. It's vengeance."

"It's an eye for an eye. That's justice in its purest form."

"You want my father to live in ruins for the rest of his life. You're not in ruins and neither are your parents," he impatiently pointed out. "There is no point to this vengeance. You are wealthy and successful. But if you continue this path, that will change in an instant."

Serena went still and he knew it was the calm before the storm. He saw the rage flare in her eyes a moment before she erupted from the water. "Just because I have money today, it's okay to erase what Aaron Brock did to me and my family?"

Cooper swallowed hard as he stared at the goddess before him. She was a glorious sight as the rose petals clung to her golden skin. Rivulets of water tracked down her voluptuous curves. She was a vision of passion and power. Of strength and softness.

"Now that I'm successful," she continued, her voice shaking with emotion as she vaulted out of the tub, "it's okay that I didn't complete my education because I needed a backbreaking job to help pay the bills?"

Cooper was speechless as he watched and listened. She moved with regal grace and potent rage. She was a spoiled princess but she was also a warrior.

She grabbed her white fluffy robe and put it on, stabbing her arms through the sleeves. "It's all right that I worked in horrible conditions and lived in poverty because as an adult I can afford to stay at a luxury hotel?"

Had he said that? He guessed he did. The wound his father caused her was so old that it had scabbed over and left a scar. He thought there was no point in opening it up again. Now he wasn't so sure. The scar would never disappear. It was part of her history. Her life.

"I'm telling you to quit while you're ahead," he said quietly.

"It's too late!" she declared, wrapping the robe around her. The thick terry cloth clung to her damp naked body. "You asked your father about me. I'm already in his sight and he's ready to pull the trigger."

"I can stop that." He couldn't heal the past wounds but he could prevent anyone from getting hurt. Especially Serena.

She tied the sash at her waist with one savage tug. "How?" she said in a growl.

"By offering my protection."

Protection? Her hands fell to her sides as she turned his words over in her mind. Why would Cooper Brock offer her anything? She was the enemy. The threat. "I don't understand."

"Give me the documents," he said quietly, "and in exchange I will protect you if my father tries to retaliate."

She gave a huff of disbelief. Just give away the documents? That file meant more to her than having evidence against the Brocks. It was a reminder that she was smarter and more powerful than when her life fell apart. At times, that file was her security blanket when the fear overwhelmed her.

Serena stared at him waiting for the punch line but Cooper looked very serious. "Aaron won't come after me because I have proof. It's my insurance."

"It's your ammunition," Cooper corrected her. "He's not going to sit quietly waiting for you to use it. Don't you understand anything about the animal you're trying to hunt?"

She didn't understand his exasperation. She had studied Aaron and knew how dangerous he could be. There was always a risk when poking a sleeping giant. "Why do you want to protect me? What's in it...? Oh." She fell silent and then gave a bitter laugh. "My God, you will stop at nothing to get me into bed!"

She tossed her hands in the air as a dangerous cocktail of outrage and curiosity bubbled inside her. Becoming Cooper's lover or mistress would put her in a very vulnerable position. And he knew that. He stepped away from the door. "Serena, you have started a war you can't win."

She pulled the lapels of her robe closer. "I've done the risk analysis. I studied the battleground. I'm in a very good position to win."

To her surprise, he didn't deny it. "But you aren't invincible."

"Neither are you. I know your weakness. It's *me*," she said with a gloating smile as she approached him. "And I will use it every chance I get. To distract you. Disarm you. Destroy you."

His ferocious frown didn't frighten her. "And I'm *your* weakness," he declared.

She stopped walking. Her toes curled against the white tile as she fought the feeling of being exposed. "No, you're not," she said in a whisper.

"I can prove it."

She didn't like his confident tone or the gleam of anticipation in his silver eyes. Why did this man act as if he could trust her? She was almost envious of his ability to offer that level of faith in another person. "Why would you want to get close to me, cowboy? Aren't you worried that I would stab you in the back?"

"No," he said as a smile tugged the corner of his mouth. "Spoiled princesses don't like to get their hands messy."

"Spoiled?" He did not know her at all. Once she had been a spoiled rich girl. A princess in her parents' glittery kingdom. Protected and sheltered. Then she became the peasant and had to fight her way back to the top through a cruel and indifferent world.

She maintained the persona because that was all the protection she needed. If it meant she couldn't risk showing her true self, she had to make that sacrifice. It was best if no one, especially her enemy, knew the real her. She had to ignore this need to explain herself, to make Cooper understand that this wasn't a ploy to regain the lifestyle she had lost.

"And you're the one who doesn't want to get too close," he continued. "You're afraid to get into my bed because you know you would surrender to me."

Her chin jutted out. She would surrender and it scared her. Cooper had qualities she admired in a man and hadn't seen for a very long time. "No, that's not it at all. I know why you invited me into your bed. Offered your so-called protection. It has nothing to do with sex."

"Wanna bet?" he drawled.

"It's all strategy," Serena declared. "If I wind up in your bed and then use the information I have on Aaron, you can dismiss my claims as a disgruntled mistress. A jilted woman who was trying to cause trouble."

He drew his head back. Her words caught him by surprise. Was that why he had made the offer? To discredit her?

"I may not have a fancy university degree like you, but I can work out your next move," she warned him. "However, I don't know why you're trying to keep me so close. Are you following the 'keep your friends close and your enemies closer' technique?"

A muscle in his jaw bunched. "No, I'm trying to keep both of our worlds from imploding."

"Don't worry about me, cowboy. I know how to protect myself." She strode to the door and opened it quickly, her heart pounding as she wondered if Cooper would stop her. When he didn't move, she stopped at the threshold and looked at him. "But you, I don't know if you could get your hands dirty just to survive."

Cooper flinched and she saw the flash of vulnerability in his harsh features. Serena realized that he didn't know, either. If he had to act like his father, would he? She didn't want to know the answer. She didn't want to turn him into another Aaron Brock.

"Transfer the Harrington shares," she said softly, almost gently, "and we won't have to test that theory."

CHAPTER SIX

COOPER WANDERED ALONG the dusty lane of the village, noticing it felt like a different world from the luxurious Harrington Hotel and exclusive beach. The whitewashed farmhouses he had passed on the way had been modest but boasted ornamental chimneys in various shapes. Instead of inhaling the salty tang of the sea, the scent of almond trees and orange blossoms perfumed the air.

He looked around the decrepit village square and spotted Serena talking animatedly to a potter hawking his wares. She stood out among the villagers in a designer blue dress that reminded him of the sky above his Texan ranch. Her glorious hair was pulled back in a heavy silver clasp and she wore impossibly high wedge sandals. Her uncommon beauty and regal stance drew his eye but it was her earthy laugh that pulled him to her.

He wasn't surprised that she felt driven to leave The Harrington for a few hours, Cooper thought as he made his way to the potter's stand. He knew his words had hit their marks. Serena was questioning her motivations. Uncertain about her chances. Suddenly the hunter was the prey. Did she realize that or did she still believe she was closing the trap on him?

Serena was blinded by her need for vengeance. She didn't see that she was hunting an animal that was far more dangerous than she. She was hanging on to revenge when she could do anything else with her life. Unfortunately, she still had the power to destroy. He needed to neutralize her quickly.

He watched her pay for a pottery trinket and tuck it in her large handbag. Cooper decided to follow her as she walked along the dusty street. The white buildings were dingy with peeling paint. The blue doors and window frames were warped and dirty. Serena didn't seem worried about the rough appearance of the village or how she had captured the attention of every man on the street. She shouldn't be walking around by herself, yet the rich girl seemed comfortable in her surroundings.

In fact, she seemed to belong in this village even though she was a member of high society. A true socialite wouldn't visit this dusty poor neighborhood and yet a scrappy street kid wouldn't glide through a luxury hotel as if she owned it. Cooper wondered which persona was the real Serena Dominguez.

Serena stopped to peer into a storefront window and Cooper easily caught up with her. "Good afternoon, Serena."

She gasped with surprise and whirled around. "Cooper?" Serena took a step back, her gaze raking over his black button-down shirt and faded jeans as if he was an apparition. As if she had just been thinking about him and he suddenly appeared. She blinked and then looked around wildly. "What are you doing here?"

"Sightseeing. Shopping." He smiled when he noticed how she used his first name. He liked how it lingered on her tongue. This was progress. Small and incremental, but it was still a positive sign.

"Have you been following me?" Serena asked as she walked a little faster.

"Are you seriously asking me that question?" His long legs easily matched her stride. "You're the one who spent the past two years learning everything about me."

"Don't you have more important things to do?" she asked, and scowled at him. "Like calling your financial adviser and transferring the Harrington shares to me?"

He couldn't do that but he also couldn't explain why he needed to keep the shares. Since they weren't the most valuable shares in his portfolio, Serena would start to wonder why he was so insistent in keeping them. And the woman had managed to uncover many of his business secrets. He couldn't afford her to keep digging.

"I'm sure we can come up with a different arrangement." He placed his hand against her tense shoulders as he guided her through the crowded sidewalk. "In the meantime, I need to find a present."

"What's the present for? One of your mistresses?" she asked. She bit down on her bottom lip as if she didn't mean to ask out loud.

"You mean you don't know?" he teased. He flattened his other hand against his chest. "I thought you had researched me. I'm hurt. Devastated."

She rolled her eyes heavenward and mumbled something in Portuguese. He wasn't sure what she said but he had a feeling she was praying for patience.

"I don't have mistresses." He didn't know why he was explaining himself to her. He never felt the need to address the rumors or make a formal announcement when he was with a woman. But he needed Serena to know that he wasn't the kind of man who would pursue her if there were another woman in his life.

"Girlfriends, then. Female companions. Women you financially support while they share your bed." She abruptly stopped and raised her hand. "No, I'm sorry, the women to whom you offer your protection. Did I get that right?"

He leaned forward as if he was telling a secret. "I don't have one."

"Shocking," she said in a playfully scandalized whisper.

"Isn't it?" Cooper mimicked her tone. "It's been that way since I met you."

The twinkle in her gold eyes extinguished. "I'm sure your dry spell has nothing to do with me," she muttered.

It had everything to do with her. How could he even look at another woman when all he thought about was Serena Dominguez? "I don't know what you've heard about my private life, but you are the first woman to whom I offered my protection."

"I don't believe you."

"Why not?" It was not an offer he had given lightly. Serena should be honored. Grateful.

"You will say anything to get your way," she declared. "You seem to think seducing me is the way to change my mind about the Harrington shares." She clucked her tongue and gave him a haughty glare. "I'm sure you're good in bed, but you can't be that good."

"Try me."

She stared at his mouth and then gave a firm shake of her head. "Unless you are ready to transfer the shares, I don't have anything to say to you." She jutted her chin out and walked—no, he thought, *flounced*—away.

Cooper thrust his hands in his pockets and watched her take a few steps. "Why are you still bent on revenge?" he called out to her. "You could have done anything with your life and all you want to do is destroy."

She stopped and turned around. "Destroy? Your father is the destructive one."

He couldn't disagree and yet he saw Serena was at a crossroads. She had a chance to pull back and enjoy life or to continue with her mission and become bitter and disillusioned. "What else have you done with your life?"

She pointed a finger at him. "Don't."

Cooper tilted his head. He had touched a sore spot for Serena. She had become wealthy but it was part of her ultimate goal to get revenge. "Why didn't you pursue your dreams? Why was this need for revenge more important? You could have become anything. Created anything."

"Because I didn't have any dreams, cowboy. That was a luxury I couldn't afford." Her face flushed with anger. "Once this is over, I can move on with my life."

"And do what?" Cooper asked. "I'm genuinely curious. You are intelligent and you have money but you have no interests outside of this plan for revenge."

"I had to put a lot on hold," she argued.

"You made too many sacrifices. And if you keep up with this, you are facing a cold and empty life. But you can change that now. Pull back and find something that's meaningful and fulfilling. If you could do anything right now, pursue any interest, what would you do?"

Sadness flickered in her eyes. "I don't know."

"Travel?" he asked. "Have children? Get married?"

Serena pursed her lips as her hands balled up into fists at her sides. "Absolutely not. When a woman marries, she gives up all control to her husband. He has too much power over her finances and her future. I would never put myself in that position of weakness."

Cooper knew she was talking about her parents' marriage. "You don't trust anyone, do you?"

"I don't trust you," Serena retorted. "Let's say I take you up on your offer of protection. What would happen?

You will make all these promises but if I don't do exactly what you want you won't help."

"That's not true," Cooper said slowly. "I would help you even if we weren't sleeping together."

"I don't believe you!" She tossed her hands in the air. "You are waiting for me to lower my guard. I can't forget that you are my enemy!"

"And you have difficulty understanding that I don't see you as the enemy."

"Why?" She crossed her arms and watched him closely. "You don't think I'm your equal?"

"It's the opposite," Cooper assured her. "I think we are mirror images."

Serena gasped and she took an automatic step away. "Take that back!" she said.

"Why should I? It's the truth," he told her. "You are fiercely protective of your family. You're like an avenging angel. I'm the same way."

She tilted her head back so she could meet his gaze straight on. "Is that a warning?"

"You can take my words any way you want. I also admire your tenacity," he continued. He thought her persistence rivaled his own. "But I think it's misdirected."

Serena's mouth twisted. "Of course you do."

"I admit that I'm impressed with your courage." He wanted Serena's courage and audacity on his team. At his side. They could take on the world together and conquer anything. He smiled as he warmed up to the idea. "You're a fighter."

"Are you just now figuring this out?"

"I find your energy and drive addictive." Cooper's voice grew husky. He didn't want to be drawn to her vitality. He should home in on her weaknesses instead of respecting her abilities.

Serena narrowed her eyes. "If you make one comment of wanting to see my energy and drive in the bedroom, I will move up the deadline."

He believed her. Cooper raised his hands in mock surrender. "All I am suggesting is that we would make great allies. I want you in my corner."

Serena's eyes widened. Her mouth sagged open as she stammered. She closed her jaw abruptly and pressed her lips together before she tried again. "Not in a million years."

He enjoyed having the power to leave her bewildered and unsettled. It felt good. "Why not?"

She stabbed her finger at him. "I don't trust you and I know, despite what you say, you don't trust me. You don't want me in your corner. You need to contain the threat to the Brock empire. You want me *in* a corner."

"Think about it, Serena. The two of us working together… I could use your intuitive mind. We would be an indestructible team." He dipped his head and looked deep into her eyes that flashed with suspicion. He knew that if he could gain her trust, he would have it forever. Even if he failed, she would give him a second chance. He didn't know what that would be like—having someone adore him unconditionally—but he wanted it with Serena.

"I work alone," Serena announced before she pivoted on her heel and marched away.

"When was the last time you had someone backing you up?" he asked as he followed. "Helping you win your battles?"

"I don't need help," she called over her shoulder.

"You don't want help," he corrected her.

She didn't argue with that. "Working with another person would just slow me down."

"Right, you are the epitome of speed," he said drily.

"How many years have you been working on this revenge idea? How's that been working out for you?"

"Quite well." Her voice brimmed with confidence. "It should be done by tonight."

He walked beside her as she zigzagged along the crowded sidewalk. "If you had a team, you could have faced my father while he was still in power."

Cooper saw the annoyance pulling at the corner of her mouth. She knew he spoke the truth. Serena was still angry with herself for missing the opportunity.

"I face the enemy on my own," she finally said.

"Why?"

She gave a short, choppy shrug. "It's just how it's always been. People have a tendency of letting me down. I didn't have anyone to rely on when disaster struck."

Cooper realized that Serena might look like a socialite and act like a princess, but she was a survivor. The glamour was a facade, a way of protecting herself from the world. Her traumatic journey had gotten her to where she was today. She had to quickly learn how to survive, but she had faced life alone and afraid at a very early age.

Felipe had a lot to answer for. So did his father.

"And just a word of warning," Serena said with a cold look. "Don't critique the person who has all the power. It would not end well for you."

You don't have all the power. Where did she get that idea? He'd let her think that, for now. It may help to lower her guard with him. "Sweetheart, here's a word of warning for you—I always win."

She stopped abruptly and turned to face him. "So do I."

"Not this time." Cooper's tone bordered on apologetic. "Here's a sure win—give up this revenge and let's pool our resources together."

She scoffed at his suggestion. "Why should I give up

something? If you really want us to work together, then I need to see an act of good faith from you."

He didn't like the sound of that, but if it would help protect his family and business Cooper knew he had to consider the option, although it would be considered a failure. He had to protect the empire more than conceal his deepest shame and his lowest moment. "What do you mean?"

"Exchange the Harrington shares for the Alves land without any delays. And then I know that you really mean it."

Cooper looked at Serena as if she were crazy. "Why would I do that? You will get everything you want and I wouldn't know if you plan to use this so-called proof against my family."

"You just have to trust me."

Was she serious? Cooper studied her intently and she didn't look away. His stomach twisted as he saw Serena's look of determination. He knew what he had to do. He was raised as the Brock heir and it had been drilled into him that the empire came first. Had he been a cherished son, a child raised by attentive parents in a loving home, would he act differently? No, the outcome would be the same. The only difference would be that his parents would appreciate what he had done instead of simply expecting it. Cooper knew, no matter what, he would sacrifice his protection to save his father.

"I need more than a vague promise before I give up anything," he said.

"So do I," she said as she continued down the sidewalk, leaving him behind. "I need you to surrender."

She was getting nervous. Agitated. Serena walked barefoot along the beach as the sun began to set. The wind pulled at her hair and her yellow strapless dress. She crossed her arms and hunched her shoulders, protecting herself from the cool breeze. From the possibility that she had failed.

The deadline she had given was approaching quickly. Cooper should be kneeling at her feet, groveling for a reprieve. He should beg for the mercy his father hadn't shown the Dominguez family. Instead, she was looking for him!

Why was he waiting until the last minute? From all she knew about Cooper Brock, he was very protective and territorial. He would have faced the threat right away and accepted her terms. He wouldn't ignore potentially damaging rumors that could destroy his father's legacy.

Not unless he was calling her bluff. Serena pressed her lips together, nauseous as she battled back the fear. The man knew how to gamble.

If he were playing mind games with her, she wouldn't show that he was succeeding. He wasn't aware that she got the financial backing from Spencer Chatsfield. Cooper didn't know that she had overpromised and underestimated her power.

How had it all gone so wrong? She knew Cooper Brock. Admired his strengths and accepted his weaknesses. She understood what he valued and how he would respond. But Cooper did not follow the plan.

Like suggesting that they bury the hatchet and become allies. Preposterous! She, going into business with a Brock? She wanted to give a theatrical shudder but there had been a moment when she had been intrigued.

She rubbed her bare arms as she turned the idea over in her head. What would it be like to have a partner? An advocate? The idea of having someone like Cooper Brock on her side instead of opposing her was…welcoming.

No, no, no! The only reason Cooper would suggest

something like that was to control her. If she worked with Cooper, she would hesitate in ruining the Brock name.

To think that she might have fallen for his idea for even a minute! Serena stopped, digging her toes into the packed sand as she rubbed her hands over her face. That was why she was becoming so upset. She was falling for Cooper's charm. She liked the idea of having him on her side.

"Idiota," Serena muttered to herself. She was so close to the end of her quest. Now was not the time to fall for the oldest trick in the book.

She scanned the beach for Cooper, but there were very few people enjoying the last rays of the sun. Where was he? She looked at the ocean but the calming rhythm of the waves did nothing for her. She didn't know how long she was staring at the ocean when she gradually noticed a man swimming toward the shore.

Cooper stood up in the water, proud and strong. The black swimming trunks he wore emphasized his lean, muscular body. Serena was mesmerized as he waded through the water to the shore.

She couldn't look away. Her body flared to life as she took in his solid shoulders and the curling hair on his broad chest. His muscles rippled with every move. His powerful legs propelled him straight toward her.

She wanted to run but her feet didn't move. She needed to leave, for her own self-protection. She didn't want to lust after him. She rarely allowed herself to get distracted by men. So why did Cooper Brock have this sexual power over her?

Cooper was now in front of her. She should have seized the opportunity to escape when she had the chance. His blond hair was slicked back as water ran down his arms and chest. He was breathing deeply, gulping for air as if his lungs were going to burst. Cooper's intent gaze held her immobile. She suddenly didn't know where to look.

"You win." His tone was low and raspy.

She stood silently, unable to comprehend what Cooper said.

"Did you hear me?" He grabbed her arm and she had a sense that he wanted to shake her. "I will give you the Harrington shares in exchange for the Alves land. And you will not use the information you have on my father to destroy his legacy."

Serena gave a sharp nod and yanked her arm away.

He shoved his hands into his hair and gave a staggered sigh that came from deep within. "I will meet with you tomorrow to discuss the details."

"Why not now?" Her voice sounded high and tight to her ears.

Cooper gave her a look of fury and hate that should have maimed her but she was too numb to feel it. "Because right now I need a drink," he said as he strode away.

Serena didn't turn around to watch him return to the hotel. She remained where she stood and watched the sun dip past the horizon.

She'd done it. Serena closed her eyes, waiting, wishing, for the knowledge to set her free. For the fear that was such a part of her to finally subside. But she felt numb.

It should have been Aaron Brock who felt as if he had no control in the situation. Aaron who worried about his future and waited for his world to come crashing down. He was the guilty one, yet his heir had assumed the debt. It wasn't fair.

No, Serena decided. It was fair. After all, she had inherited her father's battle. And like David fighting Goliath, she'd felled a powerful giant. She'd made the great Cooper Brock surrender.

She slowly opened her eyes and waited for the knowledge of her win to register. Why didn't she feel jubilant?
Where was the victory coursing through her veins? Why
did she feel cold and alone, worse than before?

And why, after everything that she had gone through,
did she feel that she was no better than Aaron Brock?

CHAPTER SEVEN

COOPER STOOD IN the large, winding swimming pool, alert and ready. It felt as if everyone visiting the exclusive hotel was here but he had found a quiet spot next to the floating bar. He ignored the splashing and the laughter from the hotel guests as he waited for Serena. Where was she?

The bracing cold water did nothing to cool his impatience or ease the grinding sense of resentment. He reached for his drink and raised it to his lips before he stopped. Cooper stared at the dark whiskey in the short glass tumbler and slowly set it down.

This was what defeat felt like. He wasn't going to ignore or deaden it. Cooper knew he needed to accept it and remember this sensation so he would do anything in his power to stop it from happening again. He wasn't planning on getting used to this feeling.

Every instinct told him to fight back and destroy his opponent. He had the power to do it. His father would encourage him to give a show of force or go for the jugular. But Cooper wasn't going to follow his father's footsteps and destroy Serena just because he could. There were other options but it was the right thing to surrender.

His father would never agree but Cooper didn't plan on letting him know about this deal. He wasn't doing this to get his father's undying gratitude. He was doing this to save his father's legacy. Save the empire that Aaron Brock had painstakingly created and fought for. Even though it meant revealing his wrongdoings in the process.

Cooper knew early on that building the business was the most important thing in his family. It was the focus, what kept them together. He had been born not out of love, but out of necessity. Aaron had needed an heir.

And while they had given him the best of everything, he had never been able to earn his parents' love and attention. He did, however, know how to gain their respect through his achievements. He hadn't just been on the football team; he had been the quarterback. It hadn't been enough that he went to the best schools; he had to be top of his class. It had gradually become natural to assume the leadership position in every situation. It was important not to look weak. It was important to always be in control.

He wasn't in control this time and he didn't like it.

Cooper scanned the pool area but he didn't see Serena. Who did she think she was? He gritted his teeth and leaned against the floating bar. Businessmen throughout the world had scurried after and feted him. They would never allow him to wait. But this woman had the power to do so and she wasn't going to waste the opportunity.

He would let her take her time, Cooper decided. She had planned for this moment for years. He would allow her to savor her moment of victory but she better not get used to it. He was surrendering—just this once—because it was the right thing to do.

He saw Serena exit the building and approach the pool barefoot. Her hair was wavy and loose as it bounced against her bare shoulders. He noticed the proud tilt of her chin but she wasn't gloating as he had expected. She looked determined.

Her stride was not that of a princess. It was of a warrior queen. He watched, his breath caught in his chest, as she casually removed the bright red sarong from her hips and revealed a tiny white bikini.

Her body was voluptuous but toned, the golden skin smooth and supple. His gaze traveled to a slender chain encircling her waist. The sun glinted on the silver, drawing his gaze to the feminine curve of her hips.

Cooper couldn't look away. He didn't want to be mesmerized and yet he didn't fight it. He wasn't the only one. Was Serena aware of the way everything stopped while she walked by? Did she think the lustful glances from the men were her due? Did she care about the jealous stares from the women?

He didn't want any man to look at her. Touch her. Speak to her. He had never felt this way about a woman and hadn't understood why men acted this way until now. He fought back the possessiveness that stormed through his body. He shouldn't want Serena Dominguez. He needed to keep a careful distance. This woman was out to destroy him and his family.

And yet he couldn't stop the need pounding through him as he watched her. She draped the sarong on a nearby chair and tossed her sunglasses on top. He was struck by her sensual grace as she approached the pool.

"This is an odd place to do business," she said in a throaty voice.

"I'm surprised you didn't insist on picking the location."

She scowled at him and took the steps into the water. "It had crossed my mind," she muttered. "But I thought I would let you have your way on this."

Cooper kept his hand firmly on the floating bar as she waded into the water. He wanted to reach out and curl her body next to his. Skim his hands along her curves and strip the delicate bikini off her.

"Drink?" he asked gruffly as he held out a cocktail. He knew it was her favorite.

"Trying to get on my good side?" she asked as she accepted the glass. "It's a little too late for that."

"No, it's not. I still think we would be good together."

"In business?" she clarified.

"In everything." Cooper's gaze clashed with hers.

Heat streaked her cheekbones as desire glittered in her eyes. Serena shook her head as if to dispel the idea. "You're just saying that because of the information I have on Aaron."

He didn't like her assumption. He didn't make false promises and he was very careful with whom he did business. More important, he didn't see Serena Dominguez as a conquest. She was already under his skin and in his blood. He wanted them inextricably bound together.

"I wanted you the moment I met you," he reminded her. "I didn't know how your past connected with my father's."

"And how much do you want me now, cowboy?" she taunted. "Now that I've got you just where I want?"

He leaned forward. "Why don't you get closer and find out?"

Her lilting laugh heated his blood. "I don't think so."

"There's no need to be wary," he promised. He wanted her trust. Her total surrender.

Serena's eyes widened. "Are you kidding? I know how powerful men act when they are cornered. That's when they are at their most dangerous. They will fight back with everything they have."

"Sounds like you're an expert on blackmailing." That disappointed him. For some reason he thought they followed the same code of honor. "I should have known. You do it so well."

"You're the first. And the last," she admitted before she took a sip of her drink.

If only she were speaking about lovers, Cooper thought. He closed his eyes and clenched his jaw. He had to stop thinking about Serena that way. She knew she was his weakness and she was using it against him. He had to concentrate on the deal before he lost everything.

"Speaking of blackmail," Cooper said as he crossed his arms, "when do I get the information you gathered on my father?"

"When I get the shares," Serena replied, setting her drink down.

No way, Cooper thought. "I've already authorized the transfer. You will have them by the end of the week once we sign the paperwork for the Alves land. When will I get the file? And I want any copies that have been made."

Serena pursed her lips and tapped her finger against her chin as if she was trying to remember the terms. "I don't believe I agreed to that."

He frowned. She had to give him all of her evidence or this agreement was worthless. "I'm giving up something of value for your silence. I want a guarantee."

Her thick dark eyelashes fluttered. "You will just have to trust me."

Hell, no. "No, not good enough. I will stop the transfer."

"No, you won't." Serena gave an arrogant flip of her hair. "It's too big of a risk."

Dread knotted in his chest. "If you break this agreement…"

"What? What would happen?" she asked as she crossed her arms. "The entire Brock wrath will come raining down on me? I've survived it before. I can do it again."

But he didn't want it to happen again. Cooper hadn't considered the struggle she had faced because of what their fathers had done almost fifteen years ago. He wished she hadn't had to go through it. He wished he could fix it. He couldn't. The best he could do was give her the revenge she needed. Make it right in her eyes.

"I don't want to fight you," Cooper said with a weariness he felt in his bones. His shoulders sagged from the weight of it.

"You say that now when you have no weapons to fight me with."

"What do you want from me, Serena?" His voice was husky and quiet. Serena would always see him as the enemy. The obstacle to her happiness. He would never be her hero. Serena would ignore the happiness he could bring her because he was the link to her dark past. "Tell me what you need and I will give it to you."

Serena saw the defeat clouding his eyes. This was what she wanted, wasn't it? She missed the cocky smile and the dynamic energy that swirled around him. She saw the tension deepen the lines around his mouth and understood the agony he was going through. It was the same emptiness she had lived with for years.

She thought that the pain she had felt all these years would somehow transfer onto the Brocks, the family who had given it to her. Serena always believed she would somehow feel confident and happy at this moment. But instead of getting rid of the fear that had become part of her, she felt a sharp, unwelcoming jab of sympathy.

She understood the pain Cooper felt right now. She had lived with it when her world had come crashing down. She knew what it felt like to have no choice in the situation. The aching awareness that you had no power to change your circumstances. She was familiar with the dying hope, the bad dream you never wake up from.

Why had she wished this agony on anyone? She wasn't getting rid of her pain but instead spreading it around. Cooper had said this need for revenge was ruining her life. Hurting her. And she saw how it was destroying the world around her. It was as if he knew, as if he had struggled with this before.

She didn't want this life. She wanted to feel powerful, safe and happy. She hadn't grown up wanting to become this destructive person. But could she stop it?

Maybe Cooper was right. Serena abruptly looked away as she pushed back the memories of despair that no longer fed her anger. Maybe she didn't have the killer instinct. Because all she wanted to do was erase Cooper's pain.

"Why do you want the Harrington shares so much?" he asked.

"I wanted something you couldn't walk away from. I needed something that would require you to sit and listen to me." She wasn't sure if she should tell him even this much. She knew how Cooper worked and would use this to renegotiate. But she needed him to understand. "I wanted Aaron Brock to know how it felt to be afraid every minute of the day and have the fear bleed into his dreams. I wanted him to see his bright future disappear. Watch all that he had go away."

Only it didn't happen that way. Aaron Brock still walked away unscathed. All because Cooper would do anything to protect his family. She should hate Cooper for that. For getting in the way of her revenge. And yet, she respected him even more for doing it.

"I know it doesn't mean much," Cooper said, "but I'm sorry that he did that to you."

Serena stared at him. Cooper was wrong. It did mean

something to hear those words. It was important that someone saw her and understood her struggle. No one else had seen it, not her parents, her friends, her neighbors. No one.

"I should be having this meeting with him," Serena said. She thrust her wet hands in her hair as conflicting emotions pushed and pulled inside her. "He's the one who destroyed everything."

Cooper didn't argue. "It's too late for that. I'm taking his place."

"But you shouldn't." She blinked hard as her eyes burned. She didn't know why she felt like crying. This was supposed to be her moment of triumph. "You're not the one who hurt my family. Yes, you benefited, but how much did I benefit with the choices my father made?"

Cooper rubbed his hand over his forehead. "What are you saying, Serena? What is it that you want?"

"I want this to be over." The words spilled from her mouth. Vengeance wasn't going to bring her happiness. It didn't make her fearless. Instead, she felt the opposite. If she wanted a different life, a chance for happiness, now was the moment to take a different path. But was it too late? "You were right. I have been holding on to it for too long. It's obsolete."

"No, it's not. I was wrong to say that. I felt that since you're a success now, it didn't matter what happened in the past. What my father did was unforgivable and the time that has passed or the outcome shouldn't erase that."

"I'll send the file to your headquarters in Texas. Everything," she promised. The idea made her nervous. She was so used to having the information with her. As the file grew, she felt more in control, more powerful. But she didn't realize that it had held her down. Held her back. She needed to let go, no matter how much it frightened her. She had to if she wanted to save herself.

Cooper didn't say anything. He watched her with an intensity that made her skin tingle. He was trying to determine if she was bluffing. She wondered if this was how his opponents felt when they played poker with him.

"You paid your father's debt," Serena said. "You didn't have to but you did it, anyway."

She wasn't sure if this was the right choice. She hadn't considered the risks or consequences. Serena was working on instinct and not sure if she should.

"The file you have is worth more to me than the shares," Cooper said carefully, "but it's worth even more to you. Why would you give it up for a percentage in a hotel?"

He was still trying to figure out how The Harrington fit into this. "It's not about the hotel. It never was," she insisted. "You have no reason to trust me, but I promise, I'm giving you that file I have on Aaron."

"Why?"

"Because exposing that information wouldn't hurt him as much as it would hurt you," she hurled back.

Serena winced. She had revealed too much. Cooper already knew that the sexual attraction between them was her weakness. He didn't know it went deeper than that.

Cooper reared his head back. "Why do you care what happens to me? I'm the enemy."

"No, you're not." She said the words slowly, testing them out. She had always considered a Brock to be the enemy and now she knew it wasn't true. It felt odd to say it, as if her mind was reluctant to follow with what she knew in her heart.

"You're giving up your revenge on my family?"

The answer stuck in her throat and she gave a sharp nod. She felt jittery and violently alive, as if she was torn free from a heavy anchor. She stared at him in a daze as she took in a deep breath that burned all the way to her lungs. This was the feeling she had been hoping for when Cooper had surrendered.

"You can't just make a switch like that." Cooper didn't try to hide his disbelief. "One minute you see me as the enemy and the next I'm what? An ally?"

Ally? The idea of him on her side was tantalizing. What kind of world would it be if he cared about her? If she protected him the same way he wanted to protect her? It would be better than what she had now, but she wanted much more than that.

She took a step closer.

"A friend?" he asked. "What do you want to be, Serena?"

"Closer." Serena couldn't believe she was doing this. Opening herself up to a man. To Cooper Brock. She reached up and splayed her hands on his chest. His muscles bunched under her touch but he didn't move away.

"Why?" His voice cracked.

"I'm tired of this fight." She slid her palms up to his shoulders. Cooper went very still. He felt solid and strong under her touch. "Of fighting you."

"About time," he muttered.

She placed her hands on his head, threading her fingers through his short blond hair. Her heart was pounding as if she was on the edge of a cliff. She wanted to take this leap of faith. She needed to see where it would take her.

Serena lowered his head and claimed his mouth with hers.

CHAPTER EIGHT

THE RESTLESSNESS HE always felt disappeared the moment his mouth grazed hers. Wild, hot sensation hurtled through him, stealing his breath. Cooper's whole world rested on Serena Dominguez. Every instinct demanded he sweep her against him and deepen the kiss. Explore her body and claim her. Possess her.

But Cooper sensed her hesitation. Serena may want him, may have been driven to make the first move, but she didn't trust him. Because she was smart, he decided. He wanted her so badly that nothing else mattered. He didn't feel sophisticated or in control when he was around Serena. His needs were uncivilized. Primal.

He didn't like how his hands shook as he gently placed them on her hips. His big fingers grazed the silver belly chain. He was tempted to snap it off and throw it away. He didn't care how expensive it was or if it had sentimental value. He didn't want Serena to wear anything given by another man. She was his now.

Cooper knew he had to be careful and hold back or she would bolt. He didn't want to restrain himself. Not when she had tormented him for the past month. He softly dragged the tip of his tongue against her bottom lip when he wanted to bite down. He lightly dug his fingertips into her hips when he wanted to clench her against him.

One sexual encounter wasn't going to soothe the burning need inside him, Cooper thought dazedly as he tasted her lips. A one-night stand wouldn't be enough.

He wanted her to yield. He needed her total surrender.

Serena gripped his hair in her fists and she moaned. The erotic sound teased him. He wanted more. He needed her to chant his name in awe and wonder. He wanted to hear her beg incoherently for his touch. Cooper explored her mouth when he wanted to devour it. His blood pounded through his veins, demanding he boldly conquer Serena Dominguez.

When she leaned into him, her soft breasts resting against his chest, his body hardened. His erection pressed insistently against her softness. Serena reluctantly pulled away, gulping for air, and he mindlessly followed. He speared one hand through her wavy hair and cradled the back of her head. Tilting her head up, Cooper caught her lips with his and deepened the kiss.

Wrapping his other arm around her, Cooper gathered Serena closer. He groaned as her tongue teased his. She splayed her hands against his chest and her fingernails lightly dug into his skin. He welcomed the sting as his fingers dipped underneath her bikini bottom.

As he cupped the rounded curve of her buttocks, Cooper felt the tension coil in her and she abruptly pulled away. He dropped his hands and curled his fingers into his palms as he tried to ignore the call of the hunt that coursed through his blood. Serena looked into his eyes and Cooper wasn't sure what she saw. He had tried to hide the relentless desire but he knew his fierce expression could frighten.

Serena looked to the side and took another step away. Cooper stopped her by hooking his fingers over the silver belly chain. She jerked back and glanced down at his hand. Did she see that he was fighting for control?

"Let go." Her voice was above a whisper.

He couldn't, not when he ached for her like this. Cooper wanted to grab Serena and hook her legs tightly around his hips. He wanted to bury himself deep inside her and watch her face as she climaxed again and again. He wanted to brand her until she knew that only he could give her the ultimate pleasure.

"Why'd you stop?" His voice was rough.

She reached down in the water and covered his hand with hers. She tried to remove his hold on the chain but he didn't move. "This is a bad idea."

"No, it's not." It was reckless, wild and dangerous. For all he knew, this could be another ploy to lower his defenses before a surprise attack. At this moment, he didn't care what her reasons were as long as they wound up in bed immediately. But was it a bad idea? Not even close.

He felt her shiver. "Cold?" He rubbed his fingers against her stomach and smiled when her muscles tightened from his touch.

She glanced back at the chaise lounge and tried to pull away. "I—I'm going to sit in the sun."

"I'll join you." He let go of her chain and she automatically took a step back.

"Why?" she asked as she hurried to the steps.

He was right behind her. "I still need to convince you that we should work together."

She stopped and looked over her shoulder. "Are you still going with that strategy? Don't waste your time. There are so many reasons why that won't work."

Cooper bent his head close to hers. "You can tell me all about it," he whispered in her ear.

"Well, first of all, you are based in Texas…" she began

as she strode to her chair and grabbed her sarong. To his disappointment, Serena wrapped the bright red fabric tightly against her waist. When she placed the dark sunglasses on the bridge of her nose, Cooper knew she was putting on full armor.

He sat on the chair next to hers, willing his body to calm down as she proceeded to give him a list of why his idea wouldn't work. He had to wonder if she had stayed up all night coming up with excuses but gradually realized her mind was whirring at full speed as she considered every contingency and problem.

Cooper propped his chin against his hand as he listened. As much as he wanted to gather her close, feel her skin against his, he liked watching Serena while she spoke. He was captivated by her animated expression and the way she punctuated everything she said with her hands. Was she only this way when she discussed a financial deal or business? Was there anything else that captured her imagination or fired her passion?

Serena's hands stopped in midair. "Are you listening, cowboy?"

"Every word, sweetheart," he promised. Not that he agreed with her list but he would pick his moment to tear apart her excuses. "I have a feeling not many people win an argument with you. You wear down your opponent. Were you always like this?"

Serena wrinkled her nose. "I have no idea what you are talking about."

"I'm sure your parents just gave in to you every time." He had no doubt that her parents were weak against her dominant personality.

A smile tugged at the corner of her mouth. "I was a willful child."

"Stubborn," he guessed. "Spoiled."

The smile widened. "I was spoiled when I was younger. I didn't have to ask for anything. My parents were very demonstrative. Lots of hugs and kisses. Lots of concern and attention. I wasn't the focus of the family but I knew I was safe and loved." Her smile took a dip and he knew she didn't want to talk about it anymore. "What about you? Did your parents spoil you? I'm trying to imagine Aaron Brock as a doting father and I just don't see it."

She was correct. His father needed him to be strong, competitive and hungry for success. "I grew up with very strict nannies."

"What about your parents?" she asked.

"I didn't see them on a day-to-day basis. They were always traveling for business."

She rested her head against the back of the chair. "Didn't you go along with them?"

He chuckled at the thought. "That would have been very inconvenient. No, I stayed behind in Texas." He didn't mind. They had their lives and their interests and he had his.

"That must have been lonely," she murmured.

He shrugged. There had been times when he'd wished he had a strong family connection. When he felt neglected and forgotten. And then when his parents were home, he had often counted the days, eager for when they had to leave. "We weren't close."

"They are very proud of you."

"And they take full credit for my accomplishments," he admitted with a wide smile. He expected nothing else from them. "My parents had very big plans for me and they made sure I was reaching each milestone ahead of schedule. My birthday and Christmas presents were usually of the educational variety."

She gave a soft sigh that pulled deep inside him. "At least you got something."

"True," he said with a nod. "Although there were times when it would have been better if they had ignored the occasion. I remember one time I had asked for a baseball bat and mitt. I didn't think I was going to get it, but I went for it, anyway. The gift I received was for a much younger child and I realized their assistants didn't even know much about me, let alone how old I was."

He grimaced at his words. He didn't realize how much those gifts had bothered him until now. But he tried to ignore those holidays and special occasions because they were always a reminder that he was not a priority to his parents.

"I don't think I can accuse you of being spoiled," Serena said as she stared straight ahead at the pool. "I get the feeling you learned how to take care of yourself at a very early age. You were the lone cowboy."

Cooper watched her carefully. "And you still maintain the glamorous socialite persona. But it's not the real you."

Serena turned toward him and she pressed her lips together. It was as if she wasn't sure how much she wanted to reveal. He wanted to pluck off her oversize sunglasses so he could see her golden eyes.

"When we lost everything, my parents were insistent that we kept up with appearances," she said as she gestured with her hands. "It was important to look successful because people would still believe we had money and power. Our image was the only shield we had to protect us."

Cooper frowned. "You have more going for you than your looks, Serena. You are intelligent and hardworking."

She sighed and threaded her hands through her hair. "I didn't know that at the time. My only role up to that point was to be sweet, obedient and pretty. Not necessarily in that order."

Cooper wondered if and when she would have discovered her true strengths. She would have found the socialite role confining. The reversal of fortune had shown her what she was capable of at an earlier age.

"But the image my parents wanted to desperately hang on to was a disadvantage once we were in the slums. It had made us a target and I had learned to change everything about me." She gave another sigh and slumped back into her chair. "It disappointed my parents but they didn't see that adapting was a survival skill."

Cooper suspected Serena tried to hide the traits that helped her when she was poor. Did she think it was a sign that she had given up? He found her survival skills just as admirable and desirable as her accomplishments in the financial industry. Unlike her father, who didn't have the courage to stand up for what he believed in, Serena Dominguez's only goal was to take care of her loved ones.

"But I found out that being poor meant you were invisible," Serena explained. "No one gave you a chance. If I wanted to get out of the slums, then I had to pretend that I was from the same world I had been kicked out of years before."

He narrowed his eyes as he studied Serena. Cooper couldn't imagine Serena as invisible. It wasn't the clothes or the image. Her vibrant energy and sparkling personality always gained attention. "So which one is the real you? The socialite or the street kid?"

"Both. My parents refuse to acknowledge the influence the street had on me but I can't erase either persona. However, I knew pretending to be the spoiled socialite meant more opportunity," she continued, squaring her shoulders back as if she could shrug off the memory. "I had to remember the rules and rituals my mother drilled into me. I had some contacts who had either forgotten what I went through or assumed everything was back to normal. It was a struggle to regain that role. But once I started making money, people conveniently forgot my past. I'm now on invitation lists to celebrate every milestone."

"Celebrations are important," he said softly. "In fact, we should celebrate our truce."

Serena slid her sunglasses down her nose. "I beg your pardon?"

"Have dinner with me, Serena."

She sat up and swung her feet onto the ground. "That's not necessary. I should pack and get ready to leave. My work here is done."

Cooper raised an eyebrow. "You're leaving?" He wasn't prepared for that. He'd chase her to the ends of the earth if he had to, but he wasn't going to waste any more time. He was not going to allow Serena to set up more barriers.

She nodded and stood up. "There's no reason for me to stay."

Cooper grabbed the edge of her sarong knowing that it would take only one fierce tug for it to fall off her. "Don't you need to talk to the Alves family about the land deal?" he asked, thinking quickly. "You should explain how I suddenly have it after you stole it from me."

"You can take care of that on your own," she insisted. "I'm told you're very persuasive."

"Come on, Serena," he said in a wheedling tone. "You can't just walk away from this. We need to come up with a story together."

She bit down on her bottom lip as she considered his words. "Fine," she said tersely. "I can't wait to see what your idea is for that."

Cooper smiled. "I'll tell you over dinner."

* * *

They had lingered over the seven-course dinner. Every taste had been a celebration to the senses but Serena had a feeling that had more to do with her dinner companion than the world-famous chef. Cooper had been very attentive and charming throughout the night. He had made her feel special and she wished it could continue.

Why couldn't it? The thought whispered in her mind and a pulsating throb settled low in her belly. She had given up her revenge. It was hard to remember it, believe it. It was a dizzying, liberating feeling. Every day had been focused on that mission and now that weight had been lifted from her shoulders. She could pursue this relationship now because nothing was holding her back. Cooper Brock was no longer the enemy.

But he was still dangerous, Serena decided. This was the kind of man who expected more than allegiance and fidelity from a woman. Cooper wanted her to depend on him for everything. That is, until he severed the relationship with cold precision.

Serena couldn't do that. She was in charge of her money, her protection and her pleasure. She could not surrender any of that to a man, especially one as powerful as Cooper Brock.

She glanced around the quiet restaurant. Serena held back a start of surprise when she realized they were the only guests left. It had felt as if no time had passed while she and Cooper talked.

She watched Cooper as he signed the bill. His black tuxedo emphasized his broad shoulders and lean build. His tanned skin seemed darker against the snowy-white shirt. She liked that his clothing did nothing to soften his edges.

Serena felt very feminine next to him. All night she was aware of the fragile straps and plunging neckline to her turquoise gown. Her chandelier earrings felt heavy as they swayed with her every move. Anticipation beat hard in her chest.

She hastily took the last sip of her wine and swiped her tongue along the bottom of her lip as she tried to hold on to the moment. She felt Cooper's heated gaze on her mouth. Her lips felt full and stinging as she remembered his kiss. She wanted to taste him again but at the same time she wanted to keep her distance.

"It's getting late," she announced. "I need to get ready for my flight tomorrow."

Cooper's gaze clashed with hers. "You can't leave. We didn't come up with a plan about the land deal."

"We kept getting sidetracked," she admitted as Cooper helped her from her chair. She didn't mind. He had regaled her with stories about his misspent youth and she found herself sharing some of the lessons she had learned as a young woman in the big city.

A sense of unease coiled around her. Serena abruptly turned around and strode out of the restaurant with Cooper at her side. She had lowered her defenses too far with Cooper. It had been a poor choice and not because Cooper had once been her enemy. It was because she never shared anything about herself. She didn't want her traits and her weaknesses to be used against her.

They walked silently across the lobby and she was acutely aware of how her dress floated around her legs with every step. Cooper guided her into the elevator. Her tension soared when the door closed. They were alone.

Cooper pressed her floor button and stepped away. He kept his hands at his sides as he watched her. She got the sense that he was waiting. One word, one look of encouragement, and he would pounce.

That is, if she didn't pounce first. Her breath was shaky

as she imagined tearing off his clothes and claiming him. She stared at the illuminated numbers as if her life depended on it. "You forgot to press your floor number," she said hoarsely.

"I am seeing you to your door."

She went still at the determination in his voice. She wanted to invite him into her bed. But she knew she would never be the same once she made love to him. She needed to walk away. After tonight, she would never see him again. Serena closed her eyes as the sense of loss rocked through her.

Cooper Brock was the only man she had been interested in over the past two years. No other man she had met compared. Maybe she had built him up in her mind. He was larger in life because of what he represented— the end of a quest.

The elevator doors opened to her floor and they silently walked through the empty corridor. Serena's fingers fumbled as she opened her evening purse and retrieved her key card. Should she walk away or should she grab this moment before it slipped through her hands? She hated this indecision. It wasn't like her.

He was like all other men, wasn't he? Serena thought. Yes, he was rich and gorgeous. Ruthless. But she was his weakness, she reminded herself. She had power over him. And she still had the Alves property and the file on Aaron Brock. She still was the one in charge of this relationship.

They approached her door and Serena could barely breathe as her chest tightened. She swiped the key card, wrenched the door open and hesitated. She turned around and faced him. He was tense, waiting, holding back.

If she wanted to go to bed with Cooper Brock, this was the best time to go for it. Because after tonight, she had nothing to hold over him.

"Good night, Serena." His voice was soft and low as he bent his head and brushed his lips against her cheek.

Serena closed her eyes as she felt his shaky restraint. She craved more. Serena turned her head and captured his mouth with hers.

CHAPTER NINE

SERENA KISSED COOPER with a hunger she didn't recognize. Her blood pumped through her veins as the excitement burned through her. She had been numb for so long. Dead inside. She didn't even realize it until she had met Cooper. This man had shown her what she had been missing in her life.

She caught Cooper's tongue and drew it deep into her mouth. He held her jaw with a light touch but she felt the tremor in his fingers. He was holding back.

That would not do, Serena decided. She wanted to feel his passion and get a taste of his need. She wanted to hear his groans ripped from his throat and listen to his pleas for more. She wanted everything he had to offer.

Serena reached for his hand to draw him inside the room. His hand was big and strong. Masculine. She couldn't wait to feel his hands all over her body.

He broke the kiss and pulled his hand away. She took a few steps back but he didn't follow. He remained at the threshold, although it was obvious by his ragged breath that he wanted to follow. His hooded eyes watched her intently. "Tell me what you want."

She gave a husky laugh. "Isn't it obvious?"

"I have wanted you since the moment I saw you." His voice was raw as his gaze tracked her. "You have rejected me every step of the way. If I step into your room, there's no turning back."

He was wary. She should have expected it. She thought he would jump at the chance to be with her, no questions asked. She didn't want his caution. She wanted him so overwhelmed with desire that he would do anything to fulfill his fantasy. Anything to fulfill hers.

"I want you, Cooper." It felt like a risk to say it, to admit to her weakness. She understood why he was holding back. She could use his desire for her gain. What did she need to do to make him believe that this was real? That her only goal was to give and receive pleasure? "I want you in my bed," she continued. "Naked. Underneath me. Deep inside me and..."

He slapped his big hands on the door frame and leaned close. "So help me, Serena. If this is some kind of mind game..."

"I'm very serious," she promised as she tossed her evening bag on the table next to the door. She kicked off her shoes and was suddenly much shorter than Cooper.

It should have made her feel vulnerable. She was used to wearing heels so she could directly meet a man's gaze. But the way Cooper was looking at her, the way he watched every move she made, she knew she was the one with the power.

And she wasn't going to lose it tonight. This was her decision and her territory, Serena reminded herself. She still had the file on his father and he wouldn't do anything to displease her. She was in total control. After tonight, they would be equals.

No, worse, Serena thought. After tonight she would have no power over him.

Tonight was the night. The only night she could have him. She would sleep with Cooper, discover the pleasure only he could give her, and then she would leave Portugal tomorrow. She could lower her guard temporarily and remain unscathed.

"Come inside, cowboy." Her invitation sounded husky to her ears.

His eyes narrowed at the nickname. Did he notice when she used it? She didn't even think about it now. It came out whenever she was nervous or emotional and trying not to show it.

"This seems too good to be true," he muttered.

"What you see is what you get," Serena said as she removed one of the heavy chandelier earrings and set it next to the table. "But this offer isn't going to last."

His eyes narrowed. "Why not?"

She removed the other earring. "Because I'm leaving tomorrow and we probably won't see each other again."

He gave her a thunderous look. "Not if I have anything to do with it, sweetheart."

Trepidation trickled down her spine. He spoke quietly but with authority. Maybe she had overestimated her power over Cooper. No, she decided as she saw the lust pulling at his features. She was still in control. She had the power over him.

"Are you saying no to me?" Her question was a taunt as she pushed the fragile strap of her gown over her shoulder. She held her breath as she slid it down her arm, allowing the fabric to gape and reveal her naked breasts.

Cooper growled at the back of his throat before he surged into the room. He kicked the door closed. Her stomach tightened with excitement as he thrust his hands into her hair and kissed her hard.

She ripped off his tie and pulled at his fine linen shirt before she found his hot, smooth skin. Her hands were clumsy, her movements awkward as she bumped and collided against him. She heard him kicking off his shoes. Sliding her hands along the soft hair on his chest, she felt the heavy beat of his heart.

She did this to him. She made him hot and reckless.

Cooper's hand trembled as he shoved the bodice of her dress to her waist. He cupped her naked breast and his calloused hand grazed her tight nipple. He wrapped his other arm around her waist and leaned her back. She didn't like how she had to rely on him for balance and was about to tell him when he took the tip of her breast in his mouth.

Her gasp echoed in the room as her knees buckled. She hadn't felt like this before. Overwhelmed. Overpowered. She couldn't let that happen. Not with Cooper Brock. He was the one man who was strong enough to stand up to her, take care of her or tear her down.

She felt her dress fall to the floor with a whoosh. She stood in front of Cooper in nothing but ivory lace panties. Everything was moving too fast. They were still in the sitting room of her hotel suite. She was almost naked and all of his clothes were still on.

"Wait," she said past her swollen lips. She felt Cooper fight for control over his body. His muscles shuddered like a racehorse at the gate.

"Serena." He said her name as if it was a raw plea. A prayer.

She grabbed at his waist. Her fingers fumbled as she unbuckled his belt and unzipped his trousers before pushing his clothes off his legs. Cooper shucked off his tuxedo jacket and wrenched off his cummerbund and shirt with such speed that it momentarily stunned her.

Serena's core clenched as she gazed at his masculine beauty. She guided Cooper to a nearby chair. "Sit down," she commanded as she hooked her fingers against the lace panties and dragged them off her legs.

She stood before Cooper. The way he looked at her was intoxicating. He made her feel more than beautiful. She felt like a goddess.

Cooper reached for her waist and she quickly straddled his hips. His hands were everywhere as he caressed her, his expression dazed, his eyes unfocused, as she responded to his touch. She knew that the power she held over him was tenuous. He was bigger and stronger and, more important, he knew just how to touch her. Cooper could drive her wild and out of control with a long kiss.

She longed for his mouth all over her but she knew it was a dangerous path. She wanted Cooper but on her terms. Under her control. Serena grasped his throbbing erection in her hands. She moaned as she felt the heat and hardness under her palms. She watched him squeeze his eyes shut as he fought for control.

She lifted her hips and pressed the tip of his penis against her. Cooper was dragging air into his lungs and she sensed he wanted to thrust deep inside her. Serena smiled. She had this magnificent beast tamed. He would do anything to please her.

Serena slowly lowered herself onto him. Her breath hissed between her teeth. Heat washed over her as he slowly stretched and filled her. She saw the way he clenched his jaw, the chords straining in his neck. She felt his hands bite into her hips as he guided her slowly.

She rocked her hips as her skin tingled. Cooper groaned and tossed his head back. She flattened her hands on his shoulders as she began to ride him. He opened his eyes, his hands clenching her buttocks as she found a ferocious rhythm.

The wildness caught her blood and she couldn't stop. Cooper's hands were no longer holding her back and instead urging her on. She couldn't look away from his silver eyes as the climax ripped through her. She cried out as Cooper gave a fierce thrust. The pleasure was incandescent as she heard his hoarse shout of release before she tumbled on top of him.

"I am perfectly capable of walking," Serena said stiffly as he carried her into the bedroom.

"I don't mind." Cooper grinned at her surly attitude. She had been soft and warm a few moments ago. Then he had made the mistake of lifting her into his arms and carrying her to the bed. He should have known that she wouldn't have appreciated the gesture. She didn't like the loss of control and power. Serena didn't want to rely on anyone in any way.

"I mind," she retorted as he laid her down. She looked mystified when he joined her in the wide bed. "It's okay if you need to go to your room. I'm not one of those women who needs to be held all night."

Cooper watched the tension in her face. Instead of being insatiable, Serena wanted him to leave. That had never happened to him before. Most women wanted to cling to him for the rest of the night. Was she regretting what they just shared or was she uncomfortable about sleeping next to him?

He rolled over, his stomach pressing against hers. He braced his arms on the mattress and peered down into her gold eyes. "You shouldn't leave Portugal tomorrow. We still have paperwork to sign."

She frowned at him. "We don't need to do that together."

"Stay," he whispered. "Just a couple more days."

Serena stared at his mouth and parted her lips. She suddenly shook her head. "I have to get back home. I've been gone too long."

He didn't think that was the only reason. She had to get

away because of what had just happened between them. She thought that she could enslave him with the passion. Only she found out that he could do the same to her. That scared the hell out of her.

"I can make you stay," he drawled.

Serena gave him a cold look. He wondered if she knew it, too. "Are you going to hold me against my will?"

"I don't need to," he said with a smile. "You're going to agree that remaining in Portugal is the best option. And you're going to promise that you will stay until all the paperwork is in order."

She arched an eyebrow. "You're very sure of yourself."

No, he was sure of how Serena responded to his touch. "And while you're at it," he said as he slid his hand between her legs, "you're going to beg for me to stay the rest of the night."

"Cooper, this has gone…"

Her eyes widened when he cupped her sex. She seemed surprised that she was still hungry for his touch. Ravenous. Her body was already primed for him. She shouldn't be shy about it. He wasn't hiding the fact that he needed her again, his erection painfully hard.

Cooper placed a kiss at the base of her throat while he caressed her with his fingers. "You were saying?"

She swallowed hard and gave a smooth roll of her hips. "You…you need to…"

He placed another kiss in the valley of her breasts. "I need to stay right here with you?" he said as her flesh gripped his fingers. "Is that what you were going to say?"

She started to pant. She punched the mattress with her fist. "Damn it, Cooper."

He bent his head and placed his mouth on her sex. Serena's hips vaulted off the mattress. He teased her with his tongue and his lips as her pleasure rippled under her skin. She let out a shuddering moan as he tasted her. Her resistance didn't last long. Serena grabbed his hair and guided him even closer.

"More," she said in a whimper as she bucked her hips.

He gave her what she wanted. He couldn't deny her this. He wouldn't deny himself the joy of watching her. Serena chanted his name as she climaxed hard. Her body convulsed as he continued to pleasure her. He wanted to make it go on and on.

"Please, Cooper," she said.

"Tell me what you want, Serena." He wanted to see the anticipation tighten her body and the desire glow from her eyes as she told him exactly what she needed.

She shifted restlessly underneath him. "I need you inside me."

He needed it, too. He was desperate to drive into her wet heat and bury himself deep inside her. "I thought you wanted me to leave," he teased.

She gripped his shoulders, holding him close. "Don't leave."

"Are you sure?" he asked as he knelt between her legs. "You said…"

She wrapped her legs around him, her thighs clenching his hips. "Stay," she pleaded.

He knew how much it cost her to ask. Beg. It had been difficult for her to admit how much she longed for him. And yet, he knew she was still holding back. He pressed the tip of his penis against her entrance. Cooper felt the sweat drip from his skin as he paused. "I need more than that, Serena."

She tossed her head from side to side. "Stay the night." The plea tore from her lips as she rocked her hips against him.

Cooper knew that was all he was going to get. Serena

wouldn't yield any more than that. And he was only human. His restraint was legendary but he couldn't hold out for much longer.

He plunged into her and her flesh gripped him tight. She went wild underneath him. He couldn't think, couldn't breathe. As the white-hot sensations washed over him, Cooper knew that this was all that mattered.

He would do everything in his power to be with Serena.

CHAPTER TEN

THE MORNING WAS hot and sunny as Cooper headed back to the hotel from the beach. The walk did nothing to improve his sour mood. He couldn't find Serena anywhere.

He passed a woman in a big hat and long colorful sundress heading to the beach. She lowered her sunglasses and shook her head at his wrinkled tuxedo shirt. He didn't care. He didn't have time to change from his evening clothes, not when he knew that Serena planned to leave Portugal today. Knowing that she had snuck out of bed.

Why did she leave? Out of her own room? He had been tempted to stay in the luxurious suite until she had to return to get her things, but that required a level of patience he didn't have. He was going to find her, confront her and set down the rules. Cooper's mouth twisted as he imagined Serena's response. Anticipation pulsed in his veins. She was going to fight back every step of the way.

Cooper heard the harsh chime of his cell phone. He retrieved it from his tuxedo trousers and frowned when he recognized the number. It was rare for his father to call and he immediately answered. "Dad, is something wrong? Is Mom okay?"

"She's fine." Aaron Brock dismissed the questions with his typical brash attitude. "I've come up with a plan to take care of that Dominguez woman."

Dread settled heavily in his stomach. He did not want his father anywhere near Serena. Aaron Brock was retired but that didn't mean he was declawed. "That's not necessary," he replied coolly. "I've taken care of it."

"Do you have the file she mentioned?"

Agitation sharpened his father's tone. His dad was worried and was trying not to show it. Would Aaron feel better if he knew Cooper was risking his own reputation to save his father's? Probably not. Cooper had been born and raised to serve the empire. How it was done didn't matter as long as it was successful.

Cooper stopped walking and turned to face the deep blue ocean. He inhaled sharply, drawing in the briny scent of the water. "I will."

"Will?" Aaron barked out the word. "You're going to take her on her word?"

Yes, he was. He believed Serena when she said her need for revenge was over. He wanted to believe her, yet he suspected she was looking for a reason to use her biggest weapon. She was waiting for him to fail her.

But his father wouldn't understand that. Instincts only went so far and didn't compare to cold, hard facts. Cooper wasn't going to lie, but he wasn't above using the art of distraction. "I will also have the Alves land deal."

"Good." Satisfaction permeated the older man's voice. "And what did you do to silence her?"

He had no idea. The logical arguments and the seduction had backfired. "It's not your concern anymore."

"It's very much my concern," his father argued. "This Dominguez woman is trying to tarnish my name. My legacy. Bring down our family."

"You mean she is trying to bring down the empire. But she won't. She can't. Serena Dominguez doesn't have that much power," Cooper said. Serena could cause damage but Cooper had strengthened the company to withstand an onslaught. "Our family would be fine if this information got out."

"The family and the business are all the same," his father declared.

Cooper closed his eyes as his grip tightened on his phone. "No, it's not." One day he was going to prove that his father was wrong. He wasn't sure if he would be an example. He knew how to love but he had learned he wasn't lovable. The women in his life had been more interested in the lifestyle he could provide than sharing a life with him. His parents wanted nothing more than for him to preserve their legacy.

Those who were closest to him only wanted him to succeed in business. And yet, he wanted something else. He wanted more. Cooper didn't realize his restlessness and his drive to make one deal after the other was to ignore the emptiness in his life. It was only when he was with Serena and saw how her revenge consumed her that he noticed he was heading down the same path. His need to succeed, to constantly prove his worth, was destroying him.

"What's gotten into you, son? Has she turned your head? I wouldn't blame you," his father said. "I've been looking into her and I see why she has the Brazilian Bombshell nickname."

Alarm shot through Cooper. "Leave her alone, Dad."

"I would but she's trying to draw first blood."

Cooper speared his hand through his tousled hair. "The way she sees it, you're the one who started it."

There was a beat of silence. "And what do you think?" Aaron's voice was gravelly and low. "Whose side are you on?"

Serena's. Cooper clenched his teeth before he said it out loud. It made him feel disloyal to his family but he knew

Serena had been the innocent bystander. Would he be on her side if she went back on her word? Cooper wasn't sure. He had a feeling he needed to make a decision before that happened. Instincts told him that Serena could change her mind in an instant.

"I know you would do anything to protect what is yours," he told his father. "Your name, your status, your power base."

"I taught you to do the same."

"You did." *And Serena is mine. All mine.* Cooper went still as the thought ran through his mind. The possessiveness startled him. But then, why else would he be hunting down Serena because she'd vacated their bed?

"Are you listening to me?" his father asked.

Cooper swallowed hard and tried to push down the intense emotions swirling inside him. "I am and I have everything under control."

Aaron Brock gave a humorless laugh. "It sounds like that Dominguez woman has you under her control."

She did, Cooper silently agreed as he slowly walked to the pool. It would make him panic if he didn't have the same power over Serena. It was a constant balancing act that frustrated and fascinated him. No other woman made him feel this way.

"Now, listen," Aaron said. "This is what we're going to do to neutralize the threat."

Neutralize? Cooper shook his head. Aaron Brock didn't know the meaning of the word. He annihilated the enemy. Eradicated and eliminated the opponent. Cooper could not let that happen again with Serena.

"No, Dad," Cooper interrupted. "I asked what happened with her father fourteen years ago so I knew what I was dealing with. If I had known that you would have interfered, I would have looked for the answer elsewhere."

"You wouldn't have found it. I kept that botched deal quiet. No one knew about it. I thought I had erased every piece of evidence," his father said wearily. For once, he sounded like his age. "And then this Dominguez woman shows up with a file about what happened in Rio."

Cooper stopped and looked off into the distance. His father only knew about the one deal. He didn't know Serena had found information about the others. Cooper would like to keep it that way or Aaron would use every weapon in his arsenal to destroy her.

"Dad, you are retired. I am in charge," Cooper reminded him. "I don't allow anyone to try to do my job. I don't care if it's a summer intern or my father. I will speak to you later." He ended the call and turned off the phone.

He walked along the pool, his heart leaping when he discovered Serena standing at a shaded bar. She was talking to an overly attentive male. Cooper went unnaturally still when his gaze traveled down her scarlet bikini. She tossed back her dark brown hair as an earthy laugh erupted from her throat.

He should have anticipated this, Cooper decided as he marched toward her. He had made his claim on Serena and now she was trying to shrug it off.

Her eyes widened when she saw him. "*Bom dia*, Cooper," she said with a wide and cautious smile.

He didn't respond as he stared down the man next to her. He knew his expression was ferocious. Cooper didn't react when the man paled and stammered before he made a quick excuse and left.

"Intimidation must be a Brock trait," Serena murmured as she set down her drink.

He stood next to her and bent his head. "Was I intimidating last night?" he whispered in her ear, inhaling the faint scent of her perfume. "Was that why your heartbeat had been racing? You should have told me that I scared you."

Serena wanted to close her eyes and hide the turmoil that had been whipping through her all morning. She didn't like how he kept turning the tables on her. How he continued to surprise her. She could usually predict Cooper's next move. She knew how he thought. And then he did something unexpected.

"I had nothing to be scared about," she declared. She had been wary but not for the reasons Cooper thought. She had woken up feeling content. Serena hadn't recognized it at first. She didn't trust the unfamiliar feeling or the need to do whatever was necessary to hold on to it.

"Then why did you run away?" he asked gently.

"Run away? Me?" She scoffed at the idea and yet that was exactly what she had done. She was so used to hiding when she felt vulnerable. Concealing her fears under the guise of indifference. She didn't like how she reacted but she hated that Cooper knew. "You don't know me very well, do you?"

He rubbed his thumb against her jawline. She wanted to pull away and yet she wanted to move closer. "I would like to get to know you better—" Cooper's voice was rough and low "—but you are making that impossible."

Serena watched him carefully. He sounded sincere. But why did he want to learn more about her? Was it because he was truly interested in her or was he trying to find a chink in her armor so he could use it against her? Was he trying to find a way to demonstrate power over her as she had done to him?

"I woke up in your bed and you weren't there," he said.

Serena thrust out her jaw when she heard the rebuke in his words. She didn't need to explain herself. While she felt the darts of pleasure knowing that Cooper had looked for her, she didn't want to get used to it. No one kept track of her, not even her mother. "I decided to get some exercise," she finally said, and winced. It was a poor excuse and they both knew it.

"You should have woken me." He glided his hand into her hair. "I would have kept you company."

Serena wanted that and yet the idea made her nervous. She could easily imagine spending all of her time with Cooper. It was clear that she should create some distance as soon as possible. "You were sound asleep. Exhausted." She pursed her lips. "I hope I haven't been too rough with you."

There was a wicked glow in his eyes. "I like it rough. And gentle. Slow…fast…I especially liked it when you took me in your mouth and…"

"I got it." She pulled away and quickly looked around but no one was paying them attention. "You can keep up with me. Glad to hear it."

Cooper's smile faded. "Tell me the truth, Serena. I ran you out of your room."

"Nonsense." She had woken up in his arms and stayed there, luxuriating in the feeling of being held and cherished by a strong and powerful man. By Cooper, a man she admired and was beginning to trust. But she couldn't get used to it. She had a tendency to scare men off and she refused to pretend she was weaker than she was to maintain a relationship.

He leaned forward and placed his mouth over hers. "Don't make it a habit," he warned against her lips.

"A habit?" She jerked back. *No, no, no.* One time, one encounter, was all she could allow herself. "I'm not looking for an affair, Cooper. Last night was a one-night stand, nothing more."

He watched her as if he knew that was going to be her

response. Anger bubbled inside her. She really didn't like how well he knew her.

"If that was your plan," he said, "you're going to fail."

Her mouth gaped open. "Excuse me?"

"You probably don't remember a lot of what was said and done last night," he whispered, "since you were having one mind-blowing orgasm after another."

"Cooper!" Her skin flushed as she remembered the uninhibited way she'd responded to him. He knew just how to touch her. He knew what her body craved more than she knew herself.

"Let me refresh your memory." He nipped her earlobe, sending a shower of hot sensations just under her skin. And still, she didn't pull away. "You can't get enough of me. You couldn't stop even if you wanted to."

"That's not true." Her voice came out in a whisper. He had demonstrated extraordinary power over her. She had liked it far too much.

He teased her earlobe again. "Shall we put it to the test?"

"No." She would fail. After a month of keeping him at a distance, of rejecting every proposition, she could no longer do it. Now she knew what she had been missing.

"All I have to do is touch you and you would light up like a firecracker." His warm breath wafted over her skin as he outlined the shape of her ear with the tip of his tongue. "You wouldn't care if we were outside, in public. You would forget all of that because your entire world would center on my touch."

She forced herself to take a step back. It was her way of showing that he was wrong. He didn't need to know how her body trembled for his touch. "Don't forget, you would react the same way."

He nodded. She was surprised that he didn't deny it. "I

knew you were a passionate woman," he said as his silvery eyes darkened with pleasure. "I had no idea just how passionate. You were stunning. You took my breath away."

She was uncertain about that passion. She had no idea how strong or how deep it ran inside her. Only Cooper brought it out. And only Cooper could use it against her. "Hold those memories close," she said with a touch of defiance, "because it's not going to happen again."

"Why?" He splayed out his arms. "Why would you deny us what we want the most?"

"I'm leaving today, remember?" She needed to get away. The sexual hunger inside her was gaining force, threatening to take over.

His features grew harsh. "Change your plans," he ordered. "You had reserved your room for the rest of the week."

"How do...?" She stopped and pulled away. It didn't matter whom he talked to. That didn't change what was going to happen. "Listen, Cooper. This has been fun..."

"Fun?" The word came out like a flick of a whip.

It was the wrong description. What they had shared had been intense. Life-changing. A fantasy. For her, she reminded herself fiercely. He probably acted this way with the woman of the week. "I have work to do," she insisted. "I need to get back to my life."

"Your work was getting revenge on the Brock family," he argued. "It was your obsession. Now that you've put that to rest, you have nothing to hurry back to."

She didn't like how he said that. It made her life sound empty and lonely. And maybe it had been at times. She wanted to change that. She was ready to live to the fullest. Live without fear holding her back.

Cooper tilted his head and studied her carefully. "Or

have you put it to rest?" His voice went cold. "Is there a final piece to your revenge that you haven't told me?"

"What do you think?" she asked as she glared at him. She had considered it but that was before he convinced her that getting rid of this revenge was the only way she could save herself. Her emotions flared when he didn't answer. "Do you think I would sleep with you if I still saw you as the enemy? That I would let you strip me bare?"

"Sweetheart, that is your classic defense move," he said with a lopsided smile. "It's your armor."

She pushed away and crossed her arms. "What are you talking about?"

"I've watched you at all the business events in the past month. You don't like it when someone gets too close to you, especially a man."

He had noticed. How? She raised her hand to make him stop. "Okay, now you're just making things up."

"But instead of hiding, you flaunt your curves," he continued. "You know men are dreaming about taking you to bed, imagining having that body against theirs. They don't notice your quick mind until it's too late. They don't notice that you won't even let them touch you."

This man saw too much. He had seen how she kept her distance from him but he hadn't mentioned it. All this time she thought Cooper didn't look for the small details. But he saw everything. He just never let on. "I let you touch me."

"You did more than that." His voice was heavy with satisfaction. "You gave yourself to me. You're mine."

She ignored the heat suffusing her skin at his words. "No, Cooper." She poked her finger against his chest. "You are mine."

Surprise flashed through his gray eyes. His mouth twisted as if he wanted to deny it but couldn't. "I should drag you back into bed and prove my claim on you."

He could try but it would also prove her point and he knew it. "Don't push your luck, cowboy."

She should have known that her words were like waving a red cape in front of a charging bull. Maybe that was why she had said it.

"Are you trying to tempt me?" He reached out and caressed his fingers along the length of her throat. The pad of his thumb rested against her jittery pulse point. "Yes, I think you are."

She batted his hand away.

"You want me to drag you into bed," he said with dawning realization. Cooper's smile was slow and sexy. "Serena, you don't need to wait for an invitation."

She clenched her fists at her sides. "I'm leaving today."

"Why?" He curled his arm around her waist. "Everything you want, everything you need, is right here."

He was the most arrogant man she had ever met. And yet she allowed him to drag her against his hard chest. "If you are trying to sweet-talk me, you're going about it the wrong way."

"When was the last time you had a vacation?" he asked. "I'm guessing you haven't had one for fourteen years."

It was true. Vacations had been an emotional minefield for her. There had been so many wonderful childhood memories associated with family getaways and trips. Suddenly, her parents no longer had the money or the inclination for a weekend escapade. Serena had tried to put together casual days out, believing that they needed some time away to keep the family intact, but her attempts had been disastrous. She couldn't recapture the memories of her childhood or strengthen the bond between her parents.

Eventually, she couldn't take any time off while she worked several jobs. When she grew her wealth, she had decided not to take a vacation because she was afraid the fire that drove her would dull while she was away. "Vacations are a waste of time and money. A distraction."

"How often have you denied yourself a day off? Denied yourself pleasure?"

She bunched his fine linen shirt in her hands. "You don't understand…"

"You had to stay focused," he finished for her. "You had to keep chipping away so you could take care of yourself and your family. And you kept at it even when you dealt with setbacks and disappointments. You denied yourself any pleasure because you needed to put all of your energy and money toward your goal."

Serena closed her eyes. He did understand.

"You don't have to do that anymore," he said quietly as he held her close. "You have the money and the power to provide for your family. You're safe now."

She didn't feel safe. She may never feel that way. But when she was with Cooper, she didn't feel alone. There were moments when she knew he was at her side and looking out for her. Cooper Brock was a man who protected what was his and he had claimed her.

"Stay here until the end of the week," he urged as he stroked his hand down her back. "Forget about work for a couple of days."

"I shouldn't." She wasn't sure if she wanted his claim on her. What would it mean? What was she gaining and what was she giving up if she accepted it?

"Let me show you how to indulge. Get lost in pleasure."

Serena sagged against his chest. The man knew how to tempt her. She wanted to explore the fullest extent of pleasure with Cooper. *Only* Cooper. So what if she was never going to be the same again? She was ready to move forward in her life…starting now.

"You win, Cooper. I'll stay."

CHAPTER ELEVEN

COOPER LAY IN BED, the early-afternoon sun shining against his naked body. He heard Serena's ragged breath soften and he turned to face her. Serena's hair was tangled and spread across the pillow. Her face was flushed and her mouth reddened from his kisses. She had a faraway look in her eyes as if she was trying to figure out a problem.

"What are you thinking about?" he drawled.

"It's just that..." Serena bit down on her bottom lip. "Never mind."

Cooper cupped his hand against her cheek. Whatever she was thinking couldn't be good. Serena was never one to hesitate. Part of him didn't want to delve too deeply but he also didn't want her to hide anything from him. "Tell me, Serena."

She exhaled sharply. "Why were you reluctant to give up the Harrington shares?"

Cooper flinched. He hadn't expected Serena to ask that question. He didn't have a good lie in place. Cooper frowned when he realized he didn't want to hide the truth. Not from Serena. It didn't make sense when she still had the power to hurt him.

But this woman had gotten under his skin and into his heart. She was his mirror image, and while she would not have taken the same actions, she might understand. She had seen how her father had made choices under intense pressure. Would she forgive him the same way?

Serena winced. "Forget I asked."

"I needed the shares to keep John Harrington, Jr., quiet. He has information that could destroy me," he admitted. It was more difficult to say it aloud than he had imagined. And to Serena. He wanted her to see him as perfect. Lovable. But that was a fantasy. Serena could never allow herself to be that close or vulnerable to him.

Serena's lips parted in shock. "And as long as you have the shares," she said slowly, "he couldn't touch you."

Cooper nodded.

"But you are selling the shares to me. Once Harrington finds out he will know that you have no ammunition. He could hurt you."

"It's more important to protect my father's reputation." He had struggled with his choice but always knew he would arrive at this decision.

"Why?"

"He created the Brock empire and I'm the guardian." He had been preparing for the role all of his life. It was why he was born. If he didn't protect what his parents had built, what was his purpose in life?

"Cooper, I'm sorry. I didn't know." She placed her hand against his chest and gave him a pleading look.

"It's not your fault. I got myself into this situation." And no matter how many times he turned the problem in his mind, he couldn't find a solution. If his business suffered, what would he do with his life? Just like Serena, he had no answer.

"I would refuse the shares but I need them," she confessed. "I made promises."

He had a good idea who she made the promise to. If Spencer Chatsfield knew he had the shares, then the secret was already out. His threat on Harrington was fading fast. John would retaliate and he had nothing to fight back with.

"John knows the details about my first deal," Cooper explained. "The one I made for myself. Not for the Brock business."

Serena swiftly placed her fingers against his mouth. Her eyes were wide with concern. "You don't have to tell me," she whispered.

"I want to."

She dropped her hand. "Why? Aren't you worried that I might use the information for my own gain?"

Cooper watched her carefully. He saw the concern glimmering in her golden eyes. Serena was uncomfortable with the level of trust he displayed. Was she worried for him? Or was she worried that the information he gave was too good to keep a secret?

"I want you to understand," Cooper explained. He needed to tell someone and the only person he wanted to confide in was Serena. He wanted to trust her and yet he had no proof that he could. "I wasn't always honest in my deals. John Harrington, Jr., had given me insider information about a business and I used that to my own advantage."

She lifted her head, her hair tumbling around her bare shoulders. "Insider... No, I don't believe that. You wouldn't."

"It wasn't illegal," he was quick to point out. But it had been very close to breaking the law. As if that technicality was going to make a huge difference in the way Serena saw him. "But it also wasn't honest. It wasn't right."

Serena pressed her lips together as she studied him. "It still weighs on you."

Of course it did. He was ashamed at how he'd handled the deal. He had sworn he was going to be better than his father. Instead, he had proven he was his father's son.

That realization was enough to keep him on the straight and narrow.

"What are you going to do to fix it?" Serena asked as she bent down and pressed her lips against the corner of his mouth.

He jerked his head back. "Fix it? I wish I could but the deal was done years ago."

"Cooper, you are one of the smartest men I know. You could figure it out if you wanted to," she declared before she claimed his mouth with a kiss.

How much did he want to repair his mistake? Cooper hadn't considered the question before and he found that he didn't have an answer. Hiding it was the easiest strategy but that was becoming impossible. How determined was he to right a wrong?

Cooper took a sip of his icy cold beer and looked around the hole-in-the-wall *petisco* bar that was off in a back alley far from The Harrington. The place was dark and smelled of garlic, olive oil and spices. The mournful sound of *fado* music mingled with the loud conversations. He noticed a few adventurous tourists sitting next to a group of locals.

"How did you find this place?" Cooper asked.

"I'm very good at hunting down information," Serena said as she smeared tuna paste on a chunk of bread. "And I was in desperate need of *petisco*."

He thought *petisco* looked a lot like tapas. The main difference was that the dishes were predominantly fish and seafood. But unlike the trendy tapas bars he had visited, this bar was old and worn. It looked as if it had been a tavern for centuries.

As he watched Serena gradually relax while she drank red wine, he realized she was in her element. She shouldn't be with her strapless white dress and stunning emerald necklace. He was surprised that she liked being part of the busy, social atmosphere. He had always gotten the sense that she preferred to be alone.

"This is your favorite food?" he asked as he stared at the octopus and snail dishes. They were good but he wouldn't long for it like a Texas barbecue. "This is what you want your last meal to be?"

"Mmm." She popped the morsel in her mouth and closed her eyes as her face softened. Serena's moan of pleasure went straight to his groin.

Cooper inhaled sharply. This woman was incredibly sensual without even trying. He wanted to feed her from the small plates and rub his fingers against her wide, lush mouth. It was a tempting thought but he couldn't risk it. He knew from experience that once he touched her he wouldn't stop.

"What is it that you like about it?" he asked gruffly.

She slowly opened her eyes and gave it some thought. "I like the ritual," she finally said. "You go to a *petisco* bar with a group of friends or someone special and stay for hours." Serena gave a shrug. "It's a social food."

Who did she go with late at night to enjoy their company? He wanted to know her friends and the people important in her life. Or did she have someone special? Was there a man in her life? The painful flash of jealousy dissolved as soon as it appeared. No, that wasn't like Serena. She was an intensely loyal woman and would not have a vacation fling if she were in a committed relationship.

But his instincts also told him Serena didn't want a lover or a committed relationship. She didn't let anyone get this close. She had only allowed him this far because she thought she had all the power. And she'd slept with him before they signed the paperwork. Cooper's mouth twisted. Did she think he wouldn't notice?

"Now it's your turn," Serena encouraged as she leaned back in her chair and spread her arms out wide. "Ask me anything."

He smiled at her grand statement. He knew that wasn't true. She was still guarded and she would respond carefully. But she had started this game earlier in the day, once he had revealed why he needed the Harrington shares. He had felt exposed and yet Serena didn't judge him or walk away. She didn't hate him or accuse him of being as weak as her father. Her level of acceptance was a gift he quietly cherished.

Perhaps she felt something else but didn't feel the need to talk about it. It was unlike her but he could sense she was going to end it all once she left Portugal. She would walk away once she didn't have anything hanging over his head. Cooper wasn't going to let that happened. Somehow he was going to show her that he was worth the risk.

"What's your favorite way of spending a lazy Sunday morning?" he asked as he took another sip of beer.

"Lazy?" She frowned as if she wasn't familiar with the word. "Why would I be lazy on a Sunday? It's just like any other day."

He gave a deep sigh. "You really needed these days off."

A smile flickered across her mouth. "Maybe I did. I am enjoying spending a day with the phone off and the computer tucked away," she said. "It felt odd at first but I think a lot of it is just habit."

Cooper was glad he had announced that there would be no phone calls or checking messages. It was a sacrifice on his part since he often needed to be updated but he wanted Serena's full attention on him. To his surprise, the restlessness that dogged him every moment had disappeared. He was able to sit still and welcome the connection that shimmered between him and Serena. He didn't have to constantly move in order to avoid the sense of loneliness.

He wanted to explore this kind of life. What he had with Serena was more than a vacation fling. It was more important than his family business. But sharing all of himself with one woman was a risk he shouldn't take. People admired his business acumen and his link to the Brock empire. If he didn't have that, what else could he offer to Serena?

"What about you?" Serena asked as she licked salt off her finger. He could tell that it wasn't an innocent gesture from the naughty glow in her eyes. "What is your favorite way of spending a lazy Sunday morning?"

"Riding my horse on my ranch and watching the sun rise." It was a rare but perfect morning for him. He didn't know if it would be considered slow and lazy. He had bought the place a year ago because he was determined to find a spot that would cure his restlessness. He felt a powerful link with the land and yet he still felt unsettled when he was at his ranch. The only time he was at peace was when he was with Serena.

She sighed and tilted her head back, her dark wavy hair tumbling past her shoulders. "I remember having a horse. I was obsessed with riding. It used to drive my mother crazy because I would be all sweaty and dusty and dark from the sun."

"Come to my ranch and I'll take you horseback riding." He was surprised he made the offer. He had never allowed anyone there before. The words were impulsive but he meant them.

She gave him a quick glance as if she didn't know whether to take his invitation seriously or not. Serena reached out and placed her hand on the top of his thigh. "Thank you, but taking more time off isn't a good idea."

"Why?" Cooper easily caught her hand and held her palm flat on his leg. "What's so pressing? You decided you didn't want to pursue your revenge anymore, right?"

Serena went still and slowly nodded. "Right."

Cooper didn't like the hesitancy in her nod. A sense of foreboding shrouded him and he tried to shake it off. Serena had been sincere about giving up the revenge because he didn't deserve to inherit the debt from his father. He believed her and she had given him no other reason to think she was lying. "What other projects do you have?" he asked.

"Nothing at the moment," she revealed, "but despite what you think, my revenge on the Brock family wasn't my full-time job. I still have to be vigilant about my financial portfolio."

"And you can do that anywhere," he insisted as he stroked her hand. "You can spend your Sunday mornings doing something you want. How would you spend a lazy Sunday morning?"

Her fingers flexed against his leg. "I would spend it in bed with you."

Pleasure burst through him. Was she trying to distract him from his invitation? He didn't care. He would bring it up again tonight and he'd get her to accept. "Doing what?" His breath froze in his lungs as her hand moved up his leg.

Serena leaned forward. "Do you want me to tell you in detail, or would you rather I take you back to the hotel and show you?"

"Show me." Cooper launched out of his chair before he gave his answer. "Definitely show me."

Serena frowned as she was caught between the state of sleep and wakefulness. She didn't want to get up. It wasn't like her. She was used to dragging herself out of bed at dawn and working continuously until she collapsed into her bed late at night. It wasn't the way she wanted to live her life but the hard work had paid off. At what price? she wondered. At times she felt older than her age.

She squeezed her eyes shut when she thought she heard the telephone ring. Only it didn't sound like the chime to her cell phone. She stirred and reached out. Her hand hit the warm but empty bedsheets.

She blinked her eyes open as she splayed her hands on the sheets. Where was Cooper? Serena went still as the thought flitted through her mind. She didn't like that he was her first thought. That she knew before she was awake that he wasn't next to her.

She slowly sat up. A light next to the double doors was on and casting shadows. She glanced out of the window to see that it was still nighttime. Now would be a good time to sneak back into her room. She glanced at the thick white carpeting and remembered Cooper had torn off her clothes the moment they stepped into his suite.

She blushed as she recalled the feral gleam in Cooper's eyes as he had taken her on the floor by the hotel door. She knew the primal need had mirrored her own. At times she felt that her intensity, her hunger, was going to consume them both.

Serena brushed back her tangled hair. What was happening to her? Why did she want to spend every moment with this man? She needed to create some distance from Cooper. It was bad enough that she couldn't hide her desire for him. It was worse that she clung to him while they slept.

"What is so important that you had to call me in the middle of the night?"

Serena flinched when she realized Cooper's voice was

right next to the closed bedroom door. He sounded annoyed instead of angry.

"Don't act like you don't understand the time difference, Dad."

Her contentment evaporated at the thought of Aaron Brock. Her skin went hot and then cold as bile roiled in her stomach. She clutched the sheets against her naked body and curled her knees to her chest.

She took in a ragged breath as she tried to calm down her racing pulse. She was no longer a scared young woman who had no power or influence over her life. Serena slowly stretched out her legs. Aaron Brock couldn't hurt her anymore.

But she didn't like the idea of this man anywhere near her vacation. From the sounds of it, neither did Cooper. It felt like an intrusion. As if dark clouds were rolling in.

"I had my phone off..." Cooper paused. "It's been known to happen...I don't know when. Is that why you called my hotel room?"

Was this why Cooper had recommended that they turn off their phones? Was he expecting his father to call? After all, Cooper had asked Aaron Brock about her and her father. Serena stayed very still, knowing that if she made a move, made a sound, Cooper would end the phone call.

"No." His tone was harsh and cold. She hadn't heard him speak in such a ruthless tone, not even when they were arguing over his family's fortune. "Forget about Serena."

Serena's muscles locked hard. Her eyes burned as she stared at the closed door. She wanted to gulp for air as her lungs shriveled.

"I've taken care of the situation," he continued. "She's not going to be a problem."

She glanced at the wrinkled sheets as the confusion and pain ricocheted inside her. Was that what this fling was really all about? Did Cooper think of this as taking care of a problem?

"That is none of your concern," he said in a warning growl.

No, she refused to believe that. She knew Cooper's flaws but he would not seduce a woman to get a deal. He would not act affectionate and loving when he was planning on stabbing her in the back. If he wanted to destroy her, he would be as straightforward as a gunslinger at high noon.

She was hearing what she was used to hearing. She had spent years looking for dirt on Aaron Brock and his family. She could always put a negative spin on their successes or charitable contributions. She didn't want to see what impact Cooper made on the financial world because it meant seeing him as anything more than a worthy opponent.

But she had seen a different side of Cooper during her stay in Portugal. He was not plotting her downfall. He was encouraging her to live more fully. He genuinely wanted her to find happiness. Find pleasure at every turn. And she wanted him to share the pleasure.

"I'm done talking," Cooper said. "You don't have to worry about her."

Worry? Serena smiled as she lay down. It may be a petty response, but she didn't care. She may have put her revenge to a stop, but she still liked knowing that she was giving the great Aaron Brock some sleepless nights. It was only fair.

She heard Cooper hang up the phone and open the bedroom door. Serena immediately closed her eyes and acted as if she was in a deep sleep. As curious as she was about the conversation, she wasn't going to ask. She trusted Cooper. Serena felt her world spin as the truth hit her. She *trusted* Cooper Brock. It was unfamiliar and frightening, and she was not sure if she should, but yet she didn't want it to stop.

She felt the mattress dip before Cooper gathered her into his arms and held her spine flush against his naked chest. Serena enjoyed this sense of closeness and she wanted more. She wanted to be so close to him that not only would she know what was going through his head, but he would know what was going on in hers. And that scared her. That barrier was, at times, the only thing that kept her safe.

But she was safe with Cooper. He wouldn't hurt her. He was a man who protected what was his. He already made that claim on her. She had denied it but she knew it was true. She was his and she didn't want to fight off that claim anymore.

Cooper bent his head and brushed a kiss against her cheek. She stirred as if his caress had woken her up. "Cooper?" she asked sleepily.

"I'm right here," he murmured as he kissed along her jaw.

Cooper's large hand glided along her bare breasts. Serena rocked gently against him as his calloused palm rubbed her tight nipples. She stifled a moan and melted against him as she thrust her breasts into his hand.

Serena felt protected in his arms. Cared for. She didn't know if it was her imagination. She just wanted this moment to last.

She felt the strength in his touch but there was something else. It felt like adoration as he stroked her skin. As if he couldn't help himself. He had to touch her. He had to show how he felt.

Cooper whispered something in her ear as he slid his hand against her abdomen. She didn't catch the words, his voice slurred with lust. He gently explored her body, his erection pressing against her. His fingertips brushed her navel before resting against the top of her thigh.

She shifted and parted her legs for him, yielding to his touch. She wasn't going to wrestle for control this time. She didn't have to fight for what she wanted. She knew Cooper would give her anything she wanted. All she had to do was ask.

Cooper cupped her sex and the carnal need pulsed under her skin. She arched her spine, rolling her hips as the bite of hunger rippled through her. She moaned in the back of her throat as her skin tingled.

Serena felt Cooper's muscles bunch. Anxiety darted in her ribs when she sensed the alertness invading him. He knew something was different between them. Did he know that she was giving him a gift?

Cooper rolled over, his belly resting against hers. Serena's muscles locked for a brief moment. He settled between her legs and looked down at her with an intensity that made her heart stop.

He knew she was giving him her trust. Serena pressed her hands against the sides of his jaw, the stubble rough against her hands. Cooper understood that tonight she was surrendering to him.

She stared into his silver eyes and wondered if he would gloat or say something arrogant. She didn't see his triumph. Excitement glowed in his eyes.

Serena felt as if she should explain but no words came out. Did he know that there was no guarantee that she would do this again? That she would continue to challenge him outside this bed? Did he understand that this level of trust was rare for her and even now she was considering snatching it away?

He dipped his finger inside her and he watched her

hungry response. She refused to close her eyes. She was going to give it all to him. Everything.

Almost everything, she decided as he gave her a slow, wet kiss. She loved this man. Had been slowly falling in love with him despite her best intentions. But that was one secret she needed to hold close. He could see her love, feel it, but she wouldn't say it. It was her only protection left.

Cooper knew how to tease her with his mouth and hands. He took her to the edge and then dragged her back. Over and over.

"Hold on to me," he ordered.

Serena grabbed his broad shoulders, clinging to him as he hooked her thighs over his lean hips. She felt the tip of his penis against her. She looked into his eyes and tried to shake the feeling that this moment was more than a gift. More than making love. It was a promise. A vow.

Cooper slowly entered her, refusing to hurry as she begged. She was twisting side to side and gulping for air by the time he filled her. The wild need inside her broke free. Serena closed her eyes and followed the ancient rhythms as she surrendered completely to Cooper.

And he gave everything he had in return.

CHAPTER TWELVE

SHE LAY ON TOP of Cooper, her head against his chest as he slept. Her wavy hair covered his shoulder and his arm was draped against her back. He held her close even in a deep sleep, she mused.

Serena looked at the ocean view through the window as the sun rose over the water. She watched the coral and lavender streaks fill the sky. It was a new day. The sunrise was a promise of a new beginning.

Serena took in a shaky breath. Today marked a new beginning for her. After she signed the paperwork and sent the file to Cooper, she would be free. The thought should fill her with joy but she felt lost and untethered. At the moment, the only place where she felt safe was in Cooper's arms.

It felt strange. After all these years she had fallen in love with the enemy.

No, he wasn't the enemy. She lifted her head and studied Cooper's angular face and harsh features. She had spent so much time seeing Cooper Brock as her archenemy. And she found out it wasn't true. It had never been true.

She had taken a decade to hunt down information on the Brocks and then she had waited too long to use it. Her days had been consumed about them and they had never heard of her. When she finally had the chance to destroy them, she had pulled back.

What had it all been about? She fought against the gloom that tried to shroud her and pull her down. Had she wasted her life on something that didn't matter?

Tears pricked her eyes. She took in another shaky breath and she disentangled herself from Cooper's loose embrace. Sitting up, she tried to push the troubling thoughts aside. She needed to think of something else but the questions crowded her mind.

She didn't know why she wanted to cry. Tears were for the moments when she had been scared and alone. There had been too many of those moments in the past but she wasn't frightened anymore. She was no longer alone. And maybe that was why she was feeling emotional. She rubbed her eyes, refusing to allow the tears to fall, and quietly got out of the bed so she didn't wake Cooper.

Serena hurried to the bathroom and closed the door gently. She stepped into the glass shower stall and turned on the hot water. The multiple showerheads sprayed against her as steam fogged the glass. She tilted her head, allowing the water to cover her face, and took another deep breath.

What was wrong with her? She didn't know how long she stood under the water as the tears streamed down her face. Was it because her time with Cooper had ended? Or was it because when she returned home, she would be faced with the emptiness of her life?

She jumped when she heard the shower door open. "Morning, sweetheart," Cooper said with a yawn. "You're up early."

Serena didn't turn around and she rubbed her hands over her face. "I didn't mean to wake you." She cringed when she heard the hitch in her voice.

"Is everything okay?"

"Yes," she said brightly. Old habits died hard. She wasn't used to admitting her uncertainty and doubts to others. "I'm just up early because...today's my last day of vacation. I want to make the most of it."

His hands cupped her shoulders and he gently turned her around. His eyes narrowed as the water flattened his hair and dripped down his face. "You look upset."

"No, no," she insisted as she tried to pull away. "I'm fine."

Cooper curled his arms around her and flattened his big hands against her spine. He drew her close and held her, not saying a word. She gradually leaned against him, resting her head and hands against his chest.

"It's just that..." Serena wasn't sure how to explain what she was feeling. She didn't even know why she was compelled to tell him. She was used to keeping her own counsel. "I want to get the file out of my life. You're right. I've held on to it for too long."

He continued to stroke her back. The water pulsed against her skin as the steam filled the air, creating an intimate cocoon around them.

"This need for revenge has consumed me for so long. Since I was just a child." She squeezed her eyes shut. She had wasted her childhood on her need to destroy. "The feeling kept building and driving me to make money and gain power. By the time I was eighteen I had a plan and a purpose. And now I realize that I wasted my life on something that didn't matter."

"That's not true."

"Nothing I did made a difference." Her breath became choppy as the emotions tore at her throat. "The file I spent almost a decade putting together? What will happen to it?

It will be destroyed as if it hadn't existed. As if the pain and struggle I went through didn't happen..."

She started to cry in earnest. She sobbed for the confused and scared little girl she had been. The tears were for the teenager who struggled to make ends meet. She cried for the young woman who didn't take the easiest path and who ignored what the world had to offer so she could get retaliation.

"You made a difference," Cooper said softly against her ear. "Not only in your life but in mine."

Serena didn't believe it. She had only been a thorn in Cooper's side until she gave up the idea of revenge. He was just trying to make her feel better.

"I knew what my father had done in the past and I tried to justify it. But you are right," he insisted. "The punishments didn't fit the crimes. I thought it was okay that I hid my father's actions. As long as I was honest and legal in my dealings, it didn't matter what my father did years ago."

Her breath began to calm as she listened to Cooper.

He slid his hand under her chin and tilted her face. "But it matters," he said earnestly. "You survived when your world came crashing down but that doesn't mean it's okay to ignore it."

Serena bit her lip as her mouth trembled. It meant a lot to her that he recognized what she had been through. "So now what?" she asked.

Cooper stroked her face. "I'm not going to destroy the file. I'm going to use it."

Serena lurched back and her feet slipped against the wet tile floor. Cooper grabbed her and held her against him. His hard erection pressed against her soft belly.

Why was he going to use the information she had gathered? That was the last thing she wanted him to do. She didn't want his life to be tainted with destructive emotions. "What are you talking about?"

"I'm going to find the people my father hurt and I'm going to make amends."

"How? Why?" She blinked and wiped the water from her eyes. That was something she hadn't expected from Cooper. "Why would you do that?"

"Because you showed me that the pain and suffering didn't end when my father gave the final blow. I have to fix this."

She turned her head. Cooper was a man of honor but this was beyond the call of duty. "You shouldn't try. It's too late."

"It's never too late to make it right."

She knew Cooper meant every word. He knew these people had suffered an injustice. Since he had the power to make things right, he was taking on the obligation. He saw a debt he had to pay. "Aaron is very lucky to have you," she said.

"And I'm very grateful to have you in my life."

Grateful? She turned and looked into his eyes. "Why is that?"

"You challenge me in every way. I thought that right was on my side," Cooper said. "I honestly thought your mission was not worthwhile. I was wrong. It meant something."

Serena wasn't sure about that. "I don't know where to go from here."

"You will find something that is meaningful to you." He clamped his hands on her hips and guided her backward. Her shoulders bumped against the corner of the shower stall.

She disagreed. She had nothing to share other than how

to plan for revenge. And she hadn't seen it through. "I'm not an expert on anything."

"You have so much to give. You could help someone who has been in the same situation as you," he murmured as his hands glided along her wet skin. "And while you're thinking about your options, you can stay with me."

Serena's lips parted as hope and uncertainty clashed inside her. "I don't understand."

Cooper cupped her breast and a groan rumbled deep in his chest. "I'm going back to Texas tonight and you're coming with me."

She licked her lips as the desire sizzled through her. "Cooper, we made a deal. This was only going to last for a few days."

"It doesn't have to," he said as he caressed her.

She closed her eyes as the pleasure darted through her body. She wanted this to continue and yet she wasn't sure it could last. "Let me think about it."

"Let me convince you," he said roughly as he bent his head and captured the tip of her breast between his teeth.

Cooper took a sip of his coffee and paused when he noticed how peaceful it was sitting on his hotel balcony with Serena. He wanted to hold on to this feeling but he wasn't sure how long it would last. It felt odd not having the restless energy coursing through his veins. He didn't feel the need to jump into action or keep up with his frenetic schedule. Ideas for the next deal weren't crowding his mind. Instead of rushing through breakfast, he leaned back in his chair and studied Serena.

Cooper liked seeing her curled up in the chair next to him. She wore a white terry-cloth bathrobe like him, but hers kept sliding off her shoulders. Her damp hair was a messy tangle of curls and she wore no makeup. She was so beautiful. He wanted to sit here for hours and bask in her attention.

"Cooper, can I ask you something?"

He frowned at the hesitancy in her voice. It wasn't like Serena to ask permission. "Sure, what do you want to know?"

She bit her bottom lip before she rushed into speech. "I was thinking about your first deal. The one that John Harrington, Jr., can use against you."

Cooper tensed as the restlessness came back with a vengeance. He wanted to bolt from the table and avoid the question. He didn't like to revisit that time in his life. It took some effort to set down his coffee cup and remain still. "What about it?"

"Why did you do it?"

He shrugged and looked out onto the beach. He wished he were in the water right now, swimming against the current until his mind went quiet. "I was determined to be a success. I was a Brock and I needed to prove that I was worthy of the name. I didn't care what was right or wrong as long as my first deal became legendary."

"Cooper," she said in a chiding tone, "I know there's more to it than that. If you truly needed to prove that you were worthy of the Brock name, then you would have continued to do business like Aaron. You decided to act differently from that moment on."

He reluctantly faced her. Why did she keep scratching at the surface? Why couldn't she accept his answer and move on? "What do you mean? I learned how to do business from my father."

"I don't know what he taught you but you forged a different path. So, sorry—" Serena raised her hand as if she was stopping his explanation "—I don't believe that's the only reason you handled the deal that way. Something else drove you to go against your better judgment."

Cooper realized that she saw right through him. He briefly closed his eyes as if that would shield him. He longed for this kind of intimacy but now he wasn't sure if he liked it. What else did Serena see?

"I thought if my first solo deal was a big success I would gain my parents'…love," he said through gritted teeth. "Their attention, at the very least. Remember, this was almost a decade ago."

His need to feel noticed and loved by his parents had been pitiful, but at the time he couldn't understand why they ignored him. It didn't matter if he acted out or if he did everything perfectly. His parents had not been interested in him.

Cooper had never told anyone how he had felt. Not his nannies or his childhood friends. But he could tell Serena because she understood him. She could help him push past the old pain and find acceptance.

"You wanted to show that you were capable of taking over the company?" she guessed. "Why? Did you have competition?"

He reluctantly opened his eyes. "I was going to take over the company no matter what because I was the only heir. And I was treated as their heir, not their son."

"What's the difference?"

He shifted in his chair, wishing he hadn't brought it up. "An heir is born out of a strategic business decision, not out of love. A son grows up as part of the family and an heir grows up to protect the family's interests."

"How could they act that way? You are part of them."

"The only time I received any attention was when I had exceeded their expectations." He still remembered seeing the pride in his mother's eyes when he had first brought home an award from school. It was the most she had shown interest in what he was doing. "I quickly learned to be the best. But that strategy didn't work for the long term. Eventually they expected perfection."

Serena leaned forward and rested her arms against the table. "So you had to go big with your first solo deal. But you weren't sure if you would succeed."

"I couldn't fail this time." He remembered the relentless pressure he had placed on himself. "It was too close to when my father had to bail me out of the Hong Kong fiasco. I needed a big score and I was going to be successful no matter what. Even if it meant using insider information."

"Did you get what you wanted?" she asked softly.

"I got the deal and it created the myth that I was invincible. To this day my colleagues think I can do the impossible."

"No, I mean with your parents," she explained. "You did this to earn their love and affection. How did they react when you landed the deal?"

"They congratulated me. And then they critiqued my strategy and told me how I could improve next time," he said with a wry smile. He should have expected that from them. "They had no idea what I had risked to make the deal."

"Then why are you saving them now? They don't deserve it. They don't deserve having a son like you," Serena argued. "You're sacrificing the Harrington shares and exposing yourself to danger in order to save your father's lifelong work. Let him take the fall and save yourself."

"No," Cooper replied. "They are still my family and I protect what is mine."

"Why would you? You are their family and they would

not protect you like this," she said angrily. "I think you're still trying to prove something to your parents."

"No, I'm not trying to earn their love anymore. I know a lost cause when I see one." Sometimes he felt a pang or a longing, but that was when he was alone and there was nothing to distract him.

"Then why do you work so hard? To protect the family business? Or to earn their love? It's one deal after another with you. No one is that driven."

The work filled a void. If he was crisscrossing the globe he didn't have to stay in his quiet home. If he was working on the holidays, then he didn't have to notice that he had no strong family ties.

"You need to pull back," Serena declared.

Cooper raised one eyebrow. "You are telling me this? You, the woman who is so obsessed with work that she hasn't had a vacation in years?"

"I'm offering the same advice you gave me. I was consumed with the need for revenge. It was my focus and it almost destroyed me. I was becoming a person I didn't want to be."

"My situation is different."

"Is it?" she asked. "How do you feel after making a deal? Happy?"

"Restless," he murmured. The last deal wasn't enough. It was never enough. He always thought that the next deal would be better. The next deal would bring him the satisfaction he craved. But it hadn't happened.

"I think you need to take some time off and really think about what you want in life," Serena said gently. "No amount of deal making is going to get you what you want."

He knew Serena spoke the truth but he didn't want to accept it. He had built a fortune from making deals. It used

to take all of his energy and distract him from the emptiness of his life but that was no longer true.

"What is it that you want?" she asked.

"You."

Serena's eyes widened and she darted her gaze away.
"You already have me."

No, he didn't. Cooper clenched his teeth before he said
another word. He had claimed her but she was still fighting it like a wild horse trying to buck off a saddle. He was
running out of time and out of patience. Serena Dominguez was his woman and she wouldn't walk away from
him. After tonight, he was determined that she would follow him to the ends of the earth.

Serena rested her arms on the table as she watched Cooper sign the last of the documents. It was hard to sit still.
She absently tapped her toe on the rug as she twirled the
thick silver pen between her fingers. She wondered how
Cooper felt. Was he just as hurried to finalize this deal that
stood between them or was it business as usual?

She had visualized this moment for years and it wasn't
at all how she had expected. It was not nearly as dramatic
or symbolic. They were at a small table in Cooper's hotel
suite and there were only two men in suits standing beside them, explaining the legal documents.

Serena didn't feel victorious. She didn't want to savor
the moment. If anything, she was impatient to get the papers signed. Excitement bubbled inside her as she imagined ending this long journey.

Cooper caught her eye and winked. She shyly looked
away. She couldn't believe she had cried in front of him
and she was still uncomfortable about it. She hoped that
memory would fade and Cooper would remember her
when she was strong, confident and beautiful.

She didn't know how she would remember Cooper Brock. When she thought of him, would she think about the way he strode out of the water, defiant and angry? Or would it be the teasing gleam in his eyes and the wicked smiles while they shared meals? She wouldn't forget the dark intensity in his face when he made love to her. And she would always long for the way he had touched and held her that made her feel cherished.

Serena wanted to create more memories with him. She was ready to start the next part of her life but she was reluctant to leave Cooper. Maybe she should take him up on his offer. She had refused to give him an answer in the shower. Serena blushed as she remembered her carnal response as he tried to convince her with his hands and mouth. His tenacity and imagination had been breathtaking.

But a future with Cooper? It wasn't going to be easy. She was used to doing everything alone but she wanted to be with him. She was willing to make a few compromises and create room for him in her world. She wouldn't do that for just anyone, but Cooper was different. He was everything she wanted in a man. She trusted and respected him.

She was in love with him. She exhaled slowly as she accepted the truth. The knowledge filled her with light and warmth. She was safe to show the love and trust. He wouldn't use it against her. Now that she was giving up the file and her revenge, she had the freedom to explore the connection between them.

Serena was pulled out of her reverie as the men gathered up the documents. As Cooper's advisers left, one of them wanted to talk to him about another deal. "I'll go walk them down," Cooper told her. "I'll be back in a couple of minutes."

She nodded, her skin tingling when she saw the sensual promise in his eyes. She waited until he left before she walked to her purse and retrieved her phone. While signing the documents she had belatedly realized today was her mother's birthday.

She turned the power on to her phone, her eyebrows rising when she saw how many messages and emails were waiting for her. Serena sighed as she felt the weight of responsibilities. In the past she would plow through the work but she no longer felt that motivated. Cooper Brock was a bad influence, she decided with a smile. She would deal with the messages once her vacation was over.

She called her mother and was surprised that she picked up on the first ring.

"Serena, where have you been?" Beatriz sounded panicked. "Why haven't you returned my calls?"

"I'm sorry." Serena glanced at the phone with bewilderment. She never had to tell her mother where she was going or what she was doing. "And I'm..."

"And what did you do to anger Aaron Brock?"

Serena paused, momentarily stunned. "I, uh..."

"Tell me that you did not pursue that ridiculous revenge fantasy that you've been holding on to." Her mother launched into a string of curses. "How many times did I tell you to let it go? You don't have the power to go after the Brock empire. No one does!"

How did her mother know about this? She hadn't told anyone about this plan. "I am not pursuing revenge of the Brocks. In fact..."

"It has taken me years to recover what that man did to our family," Beatriz said, her voice breaking. "Years."

Her mother's agitation scared her. It reminded her of those dark days when Beatriz suddenly couldn't cope. Serena wouldn't let that happen again.

"Mama," Serena said sharply, determined to get her mother to focus. "Tell me what happened."

"I am about to lose everything. Again," she moaned. "All thanks to the Brock family."

Serena's body went cold as her heart pounded furiously. She glanced at the door where Cooper had left. "How is that possible?"

"I didn't think we were on his radar but then you apparently made the first strike. Why, Serena?" Beatriz's voice trembled. "It took me over a decade to build this life and Aaron Brock has destroyed it in a single day."

CHAPTER THIRTEEN

SERENA STARED OUT the window at the crashing waves. Her hands shook as she clenched the phone to her chest. No, she realized, it wasn't just her hands. Tremors racked her body. The howling pain whipped through her and she held herself very still.

For some reason it was important not to move. Serena blinked rapidly as the tears burned the backs of her eyes. If she didn't move, she wouldn't break into a million pieces. If she remained still, she wouldn't cry. Or scream. Not yet. Not until she was alone where no one could see her.

"Sorry I took so long, sweetheart."

She flinched. Cooper's voice sounded loud. Booming. She wanted to hunch her shoulders and block her ears. She wanted to turn around and take a swing at him. Instead, she stared at the ocean.

"What are you doing with your phone?" he asked.

Serena noticed a few things about his voice. She heard the arrogance and energy. He sounded pumped from signing a deal. She also heard how close it was to her.

"I thought we decided no work until we left," he said.

Yes, that plan worked perfectly. The bitterness bled inside her. She thought it had been a romantic gesture—a promise that nothing else in the world mattered. That she was more important to him than business. She honestly believed that Cooper didn't want anything to intrude on them while they got to know each other.

She should have known it had been a ploy. Worse, she had followed her instincts and trusted Cooper. Whenever she was faced with the unknown or when she had felt outnumbered, she had relied on her intuition. But even that had failed her. Serena closed her eyes as the pain rippled through her chest. She didn't have any clue that he was going to betray her. That scared her as much as it hurt her.

"Serena?"

She swallowed hard, opened her eyes and stared at the crashing waves. She couldn't look at Cooper. "Yes, I know we had agreed on that, but I noticed the date when we were signing the documents. It's my mother's birthday." It hurt to talk. It felt as if she was pushing the words past a giant lump in her throat. "I wanted to call her." If it hadn't been for that, she wouldn't have known what disaster she had been walking into.

A beat of silence pulsed in the air. "Are you okay?" he asked.

"There's no need to act concerned." She slowly turned around and found Cooper standing right beside her. She stared at his chest, unable to look at him in the eye. "I know what you've been doing."

She felt the tension invade his body. "What are you talking about?"

"Drop the innocent act." She ground out the words. "My mother just informed me what's been going on."

Cooper reached out and lifted her chin with his hand. "If you're going to accuse me of something, look me in the eye and do it."

She jerked out of his hold and glared at him. She may be a fool but she wasn't a coward. "Why is Aaron Brock looking into my mother's life?"

Cooper frowned. "There's obviously been a mistake."

There certainly was. She had made the mistake of lowering her guard. It had been an error of judgment to let him in her bed. But her biggest mistake was showing Cooper how she felt about him. The only thing he didn't get from her was a declaration of love.

He knew how to play her. All this time she thought she was his equal and that she had the same power over him. It was a heady sensation believing this man wanted her more than anything. He made her feel desirable and special. He made her feel invincible when the truth was she was a vulnerable target.

"I will get to the bottom of this, Serena," he promised. "Trust me."

Trust him? His words were like a hard slap. "I then read the messages my father sent." She looked down at the phone in her clenched hands. Should she show him the messages? Should she wait for him to come up with a plausible explanation? Cooper was smart and wily. It wouldn't take him long. "He was putting together a property deal but the investors suddenly got nervous. It turns out Aaron Brock has been asking questions and raising concerns about his past deals."

Cooper rested his hand on her shoulder.

"No!" She tore away from him, her hard-earned composure breaking. "Don't touch me. You lost that right."

His eyes narrowed. "Like hell I did!"

"I can't believe I fell for this." She rubbed her hand over her face. "I changed my mind about getting my revenge because I didn't want to hurt you. And all this time you were planning on hurting me and my family."

Anger flickered in his eyes. "You hear one rumor and you suddenly don't trust me? I have done nothing to make you believe these lies. I am in the dark like you."

She took a step back. "Don't lie to me, Cooper. It's not a coincidence that Aaron started hunting for dirt during the time you suggested we cut ourselves off from the world." She waved her arms at the luxurious hotel suite. "And let's not forget when you encouraged me to stay here a little longer."

"I encouraged you to stay," he said hoarsely, "because I wanted to be with you."

"You wanted to keep an eye on me," she corrected him. "Get me out of the way so I couldn't protect my parents."

His mouth straightened into a grim line. "Stop trying to make me the enemy, Serena. If you took a moment you will see that everything I've done was to take care of you."

"I wanted to believe that. I kept giving you the benefit of the doubt. The other night I overheard your conversation with your father. 'Forget about Serena,' you said. 'I've taken care of the situation. She's not going to be a problem.' And I dismissed it." She was so disappointed in herself for ignoring the signs. "I wanted to trust you. I decided I misunderstood. That you were protecting me."

He clenched his fists at his sides. "I *was* protecting you," he said fiercely.

"Why should I believe that? Where's your proof?"

"It's in everything I do for you," he declared. "It's in the way I touch you..."

She held up her hands to stop him. "All of that was pretend."

"Why would I pretend when I didn't know your family's connection with mine until you told me?" The lines bracketing his mouth deepened. "Was it fake when I pursued you relentlessly? Was it pretend when I was deep inside you, giving you the ultimate pleasure?"

Her skin went hot as she remembered how Cooper revealed the wild side of her. "You took me to bed to distract me from what your family was really doing."

"Remember the facts, sweetheart. You lured me into bed."

"You manipulated me!" she tossed back. "You knew I wouldn't give you the time of day unless I felt like I had the power. You gained my trust when you didn't deserve it."

"You can trust me," Cooper insisted. "After everything we've been through together, you know you're wrong. You know this is an automatic response. Once you calm down…"

Serena's eyes widened as she gave a harsh laugh. "You're crazy!"

He gestured at the bedroom behind the double doors. "If you hadn't fully trusted me, you wouldn't have gone to bed with me. You wouldn't surrender so completely."

Her surrender. She felt the blush creep up her neck before flooding her cheeks. He would have to bring it up. "Why are you so proud, Cooper? You got to me using sex. You kept me in bed and hidden away from the world as a strategic maneuver."

"Don't make it sound like this affair was against your will."

It hadn't been. Until this moment, the affair was one of the happiest times of her life. She had found a man whose strength didn't frighten her but instead encouraged her to rely on him. She thought she had found someone who understood her. Serena didn't believe in soul mates but she thought she had a special connection with Cooper.

"Was the holiday fling your idea? Or did Aaron suggest it?" She ignored the way Cooper paled at her questions. "Which one of you came up with the strategy to attack my parents?"

"Let me talk to Felipe and…"

"No!" She pointed a finger at him. "You are not going anywhere near me or my family. So help me God, if you do…" She fell into silence as the fury bloomed inside her. It ate away at her like acid.

"Serena?"

"This must be how Aaron felt when my father betrayed him," she muttered.

"Don't say things like that." Cooper's voice was rough with impatience. "You're better than my father."

"Am I?" She felt a strange kinship with Aaron Brock. Did Aaron have this sickening fear clinging to him when his world had fallen apart? She was dizzy, wondering who she could lean on and who she could trust. Nausea swept through her when she accepted the fact that there was no one on her side. She understood the absolute loss of control and the need to regain it.

Cooper advanced on her and she scurried back. "Stay away from me!" she yelled.

"Why?" He didn't slow down. "You like it when I hold you."

She did. Even now. Even while she was backing up Serena wanted to curl up against his chest and feel his strong arms around her. It didn't make sense. He was the reason she was in pain. He was the one she needed protection from. "That was before I knew what kind of man you were."

Her back hit against the wall and he flattened his hands next to her head. Cooper surrounded her. Apprehension slithered down her spine. She was trapped.

"Whatever you're planning to do," he said with lethal softness, "whatever you're thinking, don't."

She thrust out her jaw. "Who are you to tell me what I can and cannot do?"

His gray eyes glittered. "I am your lover."

Why did his simple statement make her knees go weak? "That's not true, cowboy," she whispered. "You were my downfall."

Cooper glared at her. "Don't talk about me in the past tense. I'm still here."

"And I'm leaving," she announced. She ducked under his arm but she wasn't fast enough. He grabbed her wrist and held her still.

She looked down at his big hand. He had soothed and excited her with that hand. He had unleashed the sensual side of her and now he was trying to contain her.

"You don't want to do that," she said coldly.

His fingers flexed against her wrist. "More threats, Serena?"

More? Her muscles went rigid as her mind churned. A thin sliver of hope cracked wide-open and streamed through the darkness that shrouded her. "I don't need *more* threats. I still have the one I used before."

"Stop talking in riddles," Cooper demanded.

"You and your father miscalculated." It seemed impossible. The Brocks always had luck on their side.

"Serena, what the hell are…?"

"I still have the file," she reminded him. She pulled out of his grasp as he stared at her. "The one with all the damning evidence on Aaron Brock. And I'm going to use it."

This couldn't be happening. Cooper wanted to grab Serena and shake some sense into her. He knew he could stop his father and fix this but Serena wanted to feed the fire. "What are you talking about?"

"I haven't gotten around to sending the file to your office yet. I haven't been on the phone to make those arrangements." She gave a nonchalant shrug at her oversight but the glint of rage in her eyes negated the effect. "You should have thought about that before you betrayed me."

"I didn't betray you!" Cooper wanted to yell out the words but it wouldn't make a difference. Serena had already found him guilty. It was as if she was waiting for a reason to throw away what they had. She hadn't trusted it. Hadn't trusted *him*. Not completely.

Why couldn't she trust him? What was he lacking? He had done everything in his power to show he was worthy of her love and trust and it wasn't enough. He was never going to be enough.

"I didn't think you would." Her lashes dipped as she hid the pain in her gold eyes. "I told you what happened to me and my family. I told you things that I tried to forget."

He knew how hard it had been for her to share those moments. Serena told them in the dark of night. She had whispered as if she was making a confession. She had been turned away from him but still in his arms. As difficult as it was to hear her stories, Cooper had been honored that she'd shared them with him. And now she regretted it.

"I didn't tell you it for sympathy." Her voice cracked and he saw the tears in her eyes. "I told you because those challenges shaped me. I wanted you to understand why I am the way I am."

"I know." He understood that her need for revenge was really a need to take control of her life.

She flattened her hand against her chest. "And you used it against me."

Cooper flinched. Her words were like a jagged dagger to the heart. How could she think he would do this to her? "No."

She hastily wiped her fingertips under her eye. "I didn't realize my pain would give you inspiration."

"I'm not that kind of man." He felt sick that Serena would think that. He had shown her a side of himself that no one else saw. The vulnerable side that needed love and understanding. What had she seen in him that made her think he wanted her to suffer? "You, of all people, should know that."

"This is what I know." Her voice was laden with disappointment. "You learned all the tricks of the trade from your father. You also will do anything to win and to protect your family."

"That's not true." It had been once. When building the family empire was the only thing in his life. But that had changed.

"Right, right." She gave a dismissive wave of her hand. "You won't break the law. You will seduce me, bed me, twist me inside out…"

"You were the seductress." He would never forget the way she'd stripped her clothes off as she invited him into her bed. She could not take that away from him.

Her cheeks were bright red but she didn't look away. "Don't act like you're the innocent bystander, Cooper. It doesn't suit you."

"And don't act so cold with me." His hand gripped her wrist tighter. "We both know that's a lie."

She leaned forward. "Believe me, you will prefer the coldness to the rage."

"Show me the rage. I can take it." He didn't want her to hide anything from him. He wanted to know everything she was feeling. Understand what was going on in her mind. Find out why she thought he was untrustworthy.

He saw the twitch at her mouth and the fire in her eyes. He wanted her to break past the barrier and stop protecting herself against him.

Her eyes narrowed. "Whatever I felt about you is gone."

Cooper clenched his teeth. Her words pricked at the fear deep inside him. That he was unlovable. That there was something inherently wrong with him and he didn't deserve to be loved or feel affection. Serena didn't love him. Didn't trust him. Instead, she wanted to immediately discard what they had.

He refused to believe that what he shared with Serena was that weak and temporary. He wanted to prove that what they had was still there. "I'm warning you, Serena."

"Or what?" she said. "What could you possibly do that you haven't done already? And to think I shared my bed with you. My body. My h—"

His mouth went crashing down on hers. Cooper knew he was losing her and this was the only hold he had over Serena. He gripped the back of her head and poured everything he felt into the kiss. The desperation, the love, the desire and the fear.

She bit down on his lip and Cooper yanked his head back. His lip throbbed as he stared at her flushed face. Serena's eyes were big and wild.

"Let go of me right now," she ordered.

"I can't," he confessed in a hoarse whisper. If he let go, she would be gone forever. He belonged to her and she didn't want him. "Not until you see the truth."

"You mean your version of the truth." She pulled away from him and marched to the door. "Is this where you tell me how much you want to take care of me? Is this your idea of protection? And you wonder why I didn't take you up on your offer."

"You didn't accept my offer because you couldn't allow yourself to rely on a man. Especially me." His shoulders slumped in defeat. "Nothing I say or do will change your mind because you are caught in the past." He wanted to go after her but it would only make it worse. "I should have known that you gave up too easily. You were just waiting for an excuse to continue. It didn't matter how small or flimsy one might be."

"Flimsy?" She almost choked on the word. Serena whirled around. "You are trying to wreck my family's livelihood. *Again.* You're trying to return me to the violent, filthy and hopeless world. Do you think that will make me weak? Scared?"

"No," he said as he studied her. Serena stood tall and proud before him even in defeat. Her chin was thrust out in defiance and her eyes flashed with cold fury. "That place makes you angry and even more determined."

"So you do understand me." Serena opened the door and looked over her shoulder. "Get ready for a storm, Cooper, because I'm going to unleash everything I have on you."

CHAPTER FOURTEEN

SERENA STARED AT the signature line of the document. This was the last step to finalize her deal. Why was she disappointed that there was nothing more? It didn't make sense.

She pressed the fountain pen on the thick paper and signed her name with a flourish. *There.* She tossed down the pen and leaned back in the chair. She had done it. She had transferred the Harrington shares to Spencer Chatsfield.

Serena folded her hands in her lap and twisted the oversize ring around her finger. She glanced at the Brazilian citrine stone but the talisman did nothing for her this time. She remembered when her mother had worn the cocktail ring at glamorous parties while reigning over her social world. It had been Beatriz's goal. Her dream come true. Serena always associated the yellow gem with achievement.

She should be proud of her achievement. It had been touch and go but she had fulfilled her promise. She had done something that almost no one believed she could accomplish. She had snatched the Harrington shares away from Cooper Brock. Made him yield to her command because there was nothing he could do about it.

So why didn't she feel triumphant? The thrill of victory didn't strum through her veins. If anything, she felt broken and alone. Tired.

Serena closed her eyes and tried to shore up her remaining strength. It had been a difficult week. Beatriz Dominguez had been hysterical at the mere thought of Aaron Brock. Her wealthy benefactor had not been understanding and did not care for Beatriz's dramatic behavior. Serena was grateful that she had missed the epic argument that led to Beatriz's breakup but she wished she had been there for her mother. She had promised to protect and care for her parents and forgot about that when she went after the Brock empire.

But if there was one thing Serena had learned from her parents, it was to keep up the image. She lifted her chin and rolled back her shoulders. *Always look more successful than you are. Show confidence when you feel insecure.* She gave a warm smile even though she felt empty inside. *Don't let anyone see you cry.*

"Congratulations, Spencer." She was impressed that her husky voice didn't betray her inner turmoil.

"Thank you." Spencer Chatsfield smiled. Serena noticed he was handsome but she didn't find him as fascinating as Cooper Brock. "Shall we have a toast to our success?"

"I wish I could but I have another appointment," Serena lied as she reached for her purse and rose from her chair. She had to get back to her mother, who had taken to her bed. Serena was determined to give her the best care she needed immediately. It felt as if history was repeating itself but she would not allow the results to be the same. This time she wasn't going to wait and hope for the best. She wouldn't pray that someone would save them. She would protect her family from falling back into hell even if her parents didn't think she had the power to do so. Despite

Serena's assurances that she would always take care of her mother, Beatriz was deeply concerned about her future now that she didn't have a man supporting her.

"Another time, then." Spencer stood up. "I'm impressed, Serena. You managed to get these shares in record time."

"I had done my research." Or thought she did. What was it that Cooper had said? She hadn't understood the animal she was hunting. Aaron she understood, but Cooper was different. She thought he wouldn't use the passion and love she felt for him. She believed she could trust him. He had been her weakness. Her blind spot. Just as he had planned.

"I hope we will do business together in the future," Spencer interrupted her thoughts.

Serena gave a sharp nod but didn't say anything. She may have given that as the reason for doing this deal but it didn't interest her. This kind of cutthroat business wasn't for her. Cooper had been correct: this revenge had almost been her undoing.

He and his father had been very close to destroying her family for a second time. And then, quite suddenly, they had stopped. She knew that was Cooper's doing. Aaron would have continued until there was nothing left.

Why did Cooper stop his father? Was he flexing his muscles, showing what he could do on a whim? Did he no longer care because he had other priorities? Or was this the calm before the storm?

Serena was worried, bracing herself for the next onslaught. Her mother was shaken and Felipe had been furious that she had continued the battle for revenge. Beatriz blamed her for her current predicament. The constant refrain she had heard for the past few days was why couldn't she have left it alone.

She wished she had. Serena knew it could have been

worse. She still had her money and her home. And yet, she wished she had never met Cooper Brock. Her instincts had failed her. She'd finally given her trust and her heart but it was to the wrong man.

"How did you get Cooper to let go of the shares?" Spencer asked as he escorted her to the door. "A piece of The Harrington is a good investment."

"I had leverage." She paused as the hurt and anger pressed against her chest. All those years of gathering the information and it only caused her family more grief. "Ammunition."

Spencer's blue eyes narrowed. "What kind of ammunition? Brock is a respected businessman."

Have you looked closely at his first deal? And how much do you know about his father? The questions tingled at the tip of her tongue. Serena parted her lips and stopped.

Why was she hesitating? She would only be telling the truth. This was her chance to hurt Cooper the way he had hurt her. All she had to do was share what she knew about Aaron Brock. She could produce the evidence if she needed to.

"Cooper will do anything to protect what is his," she began as her heart began to pound. This wasn't a huge revelation. Everyone knew that Cooper Brock was territorial and possessive. And yet she felt disloyal for even saying it.

"Whatever you had must have been a real threat. I'm sure he didn't surrender these shares easily."

"No, he didn't." She still remembered the look on Cooper's face when they were in the pool. The defeat had extinguished the twinkle in his silver eyes. The agony was stamped on his face. It had been like a punch to her chest because she remembered how it felt to be that vulnerable. She hadn't wanted to be the cause of such pain.

She could tell herself that she didn't want to lower herself to Aaron Brock's level but it was more than that. She didn't want to hurt Cooper. Today she could convince herself that revealing the secrets would be just. It was an eye for an eye. Cooper deserved it and he had brought it on himself.

But she couldn't destroy him.

Pain radiated from Serena. Cooper had taken advantage of her feelings and tempted her with an idyllic love affair. But there was no love, at least not on his part.

"What was the ammunition?" Spencer asked.

She recalled the thick file that was tucked away in her home. The brown folder was creased and worn in some places. It represented years of work. Why not use it? Why not flex her muscles and show Cooper she couldn't be destroyed?

No, she was ending this now. It was the only way to move on and to heal. Serena gave a shake to her head. "It doesn't matter anymore. It no longer exists."

Spencer frowned. "What do you mean?"

She shrugged and wished she hadn't brought it up. Even now, after Cooper had betrayed her, she still felt the need to protect him. She loved him when she shouldn't. "I used it to make this deal happen and it's gone now. And everyone gets what they wanted. I call this a success."

"I got the shares and Cooper got the Alves land deal. What did you get?"

"What I deserved." She gave a tight smile as the pain inside her intensified. "Goodbye, Spencer. I look forward to working with you again."

He shook her hand and let her out of his office. She wasn't sure what Spencer said as she focused on ignoring the pain. When he went back into his office and closed the door, Serena paused to retrieve her cell phone. She was sure her mother had left several messages.

"John, Jr.?" she heard Spencer say in his office. "Spencer Chatsfield. I'm calling to buy your remaining shares of The Harrington."

Serena tilted her head closer to the door.

"Yes, I said remaining shares. I just bought the shares that Cooper Brock won from you at the poker game. Now my shares match Isabelle's, I have every faith I can win over the last shareholder with the final two percent. The Harrington will become the latest Chatsfield acquisition."

Serena bit her bottom lip when she heard Spencer's victorious laugh and immediately walked away from the door. What was going to happen next? John Harrington, Jr., knew Cooper no longer had the shares. He could spill all his secrets about Cooper. How would Cooper protect himself?

She shook her head. She shouldn't care how this affected Cooper. He would find a way to protect himself and his company. She couldn't afford to care about Cooper Brock. The man betrayed her and she was concerned about him. When would she ever learn? It was time for her to move on, once and for all.

"Cooper?"

Cooper heard Aaron Brock's deep scratchy voice ring through his home followed by the clomp of heavy boots. He stepped out of his office and saw his father stride down the corridor. The older man wore a blue flannel shirt and faded jeans. He had taken off his cowboy hat and was ruffling his hand through his short gray hair.

Once again he was struck by the similarities he shared with his father. They were both tall and lean. Everyone knew where Cooper inherited the silver eyes and hooked nose. But the lines crisscrossing Aaron Brock's tanned face told a story of struggle and sacrifice.

"Hi, Dad." Cooper leaned against the door frame as his father approached. "Glad you could make it."

"What in tarnation is going on? I flew down here as fast as I could." Aaron's mouth twisted. "I actually get to step foot in your ranch? Hell must have frozen over."

Cooper gave a deep sigh. He didn't know how many times he had to explain this to his father. "You were never banned, Dad. You've been to my other homes."

"But never this one," Aaron pointed out. He stepped into the office and looked around with a deep curiosity. He wrinkled his nose at the clean, contemporary lines of the room and the modern furniture.

Cooper followed him. He wasn't going to explain that this house was different. It wasn't the townhome he had in the city where he entertained clients and colleagues. It wasn't like the penthouse apartments he had around the world that were places he could stay while he traveled. This place was his sanctuary. No one but Serena had been invited to stay.

Serena. Cooper closed his eyes. He suddenly remembered how she looked sleeping in his bed. Her dark brown hair fanned the pillow, her arms and legs sprawled across the mattress in wild abandon. She had stolen most of the sheets during the night and they had twisted around her naked body. But what he remembered most was that she had appeared soft and trusting. Peaceful and beautiful.

His father stood at the wall of windows and studied Cooper's land. His ranch went as far as the eye could see. Aaron gave a nod of approval and turned to his son. "So what's the urgency?"

Cooper walked over to his sleek wood desk. It was almost bare, with the exception of his laptop computer and an old brown folder that was bulging at the worn seams. "Serena Dominguez sent me the file she had on you."

When he had seen the file, with no letter, nothing personal, he knew this wasn't a grand gesture of love. It wasn't even an act of surrender or a show of trust. Serena was making it very clear that any business they had was finished. She was severing their connection.

Aaron's smile split his weathered face. He tossed his hat on the desk, the crown upside down. "Good. I told you she needed a scare."

Anger billowed in Cooper's chest and he took a deep breath. He wasn't going to get into a shouting match with his father. He had to show where Aaron went wrong and how it could never happen again.

"No," Cooper bit out, "that scare almost cost you. I'm surprised she didn't release the information the minute she found out what you had done behind my back."

"Behind your back?" Aaron gave him a dark look. "I was protecting you. Protecting this family."

Cooper shoved his hands in his hair. Aaron Brock was protecting his legacy, nothing more. "I told you that I had everything under control. You undermined my authority."

"Authority?" Aaron gave a snort. "That Dominguez woman had you wrapped around her little finger. She was going to dangle the file and have you jump every time she gave an order."

Cooper had been spellbound and he'd had no interest in breaking it. He also knew that Serena was under his spell. It was a constant balancing act but he didn't think she would use her power against him. She had trusted him and, with a woman like Serena, along came love. She had never said it, but he knew.

But that could be wishful thinking on his part. She wasn't reacting as he thought she would. He knew Serena wouldn't betray him unless she felt threatened. She had been under attack and instead of confronting him, fighting tooth and nail, Serena had been silent and kept her distance.

"What took her so long to send the file?" Aaron asked as he grabbed the file and opened it. "And why did she mail it to your ranch?"

Cooper crossed his arms, fighting the instinct to snatch the folder away. "She sent it here so there was less chance of someone opening the package and reading the damning evidence."

"Is that what she told you?" Aaron murmured. He was distracted as he skimmed through the papers.

"I haven't spoken to her since we were in Portugal." Maybe he was reading too much into her choices. But he knew deep in his bones that Serena was shielding him even when she had the urge to destroy him.

Cooper reached out and splayed his hand on the folder. This file belonged to him now. It wasn't his father's. Serena had given it to him to either safeguard the information or destroy it.

Aaron glanced up. "What's going on, Cooper?"

"Did you know what happened to Serena after you destroyed her father's business? What happened to her family?"

His father rolled his eyes. "I don't know what sob story she told you…"

"What about the other businesses you crushed? What happened to those men and their families?"

"What about them?" His father gave him a warning look. "All of those guys tried to hurt us. They deserved payback."

"You're wrong. They deserve reparation."

Aaron's mouth dropped open. "Have you lost your mind?"

He probably had. He hadn't thought this way until Serena had gotten into his head. Until he saw her point of view. Cooper always had a problem with the way his father demolished these companies. It didn't sit right with his sense of justice but he chose to ignore it. He was ashamed of his lack of action. That wasn't the kind of man he wanted to be.

"Are you proud of how you handled these deals?" he asked his father.

The older man slowly sat down on the chair next to him. "No."

He was surprised that his father admitted that out loud. "We've done an injustice to these men and we are going to fix that."

Aaron was already shaking his head. "We can't. It's too late. Some of these deals happened too long ago."

"I still have to try."

Aaron slapped the folder closed. "What did that Dominguez woman do to you?"

Cooper clenched his teeth. "Her name is Serena."

"I knew she was trouble the moment you mentioned her." He looked down at the folder and scowled. "Her father wasn't a victim, you know. He wasn't a good guy."

"Neither were we."

Aaron slumped in his chair. He suddenly looked much older than his years. "I was protecting us. We could have been the ones who lost everything."

"You're exaggerating," Cooper said. "We would have been wounded. Weakened. But lose everything? You were smarter than that. You wouldn't have built a business that would have lost everything over one bad deal."

"That may be true," Aaron said before lapsing into silence. "And...I may have overreacted when that Dominguez woman threatened to expose us. But I pulled back when you told me to."

It wasn't fast enough. The damage was already done. Serena thought Cooper had planned it all along. It angered him that Serena didn't trust him and yet he knew it looked bad. There was no way he could prove that he was blind-sided by his father's actions.

"What is it about this…Serena?" Aaron asked.

Cooper didn't know how to explain it. Serena was just like him. They understood each other. They challenged each other. She was the one person he shouldn't trust and yet she was the only one he wanted to be with. For a moment, he had thought she had the strength to love him. Now he knew that wasn't going to happen, but that didn't stop him from wanting to care for her.

"She's mine," he finally said. "I protect what is mine."

Aaron raised an eyebrow. "You would choose her over your family? Your own flesh and blood?"

He glanced at the file and then at his father. "Yes. In fact, I'm keeping that file under lock and key. If you try to hurt Serena or her family, you won't have to worry about any Dominguez releasing that information because I will!"

CHAPTER FIFTEEN

THIS COULDN'T BE the right place. Cooper stood at the edge of the broken sidewalk and looked around. He had been to Brazil before but not in a neighborhood like this. The buildings were built so close that they appeared on top of one another.

Cooper removed his sunglasses and stared at the storefront. There was no sign and no splash of color. There was nothing that indicated Serena's ownership.

He looked around the street. This was the neighborhood Serena had grown up in after her parents had lost everything. He tried to imagine a spoiled teenager being tossed into this new world. She had taken the luxury and protection for granted and then spent over a decade trying to regain it. How had she survived? How did she get out? Any idealism would have been crushed by the overwhelming sense of resignation lingering in the air.

He would never call her a spoiled princess again. He had taken one look at her glamorous appearance and made a snap judgment. Serena had more courage than he thought was possible. She was stronger than even she imagined. Serena Dominguez was no damsel in distress. She truly was a warrior.

He squared his shoulders back and strode inside the small office. The place was clean but plain with white

walls and a linoleum floor. There were a few people in
the waiting area sitting on folded metal chairs and filling
out forms. Serena was nowhere around.

A young woman sitting behind the front desk glanced
up. She froze and slowly took in his appearance. He knew
he looked out of place in his black pinstripe suit and silk
red tie. He had dressed to impress his sophisticated Serena.

"I'm looking for Serena Dominguez," he said.

The woman frowned and gave a rapid reply. He didn't
understand a word.

"Serena Dominguez," he repeated louder.

The woman continued to speak while gesturing with
her hands. Was he in the right place? Was this woman the
receptionist? He really needed to learn Portuguese if he
was going to have Serena in his life. And he would.

He heard a door swing open at the far end of the
room and hit the wall behind it. Cooper turned, his heart
clenching as he saw Serena at the doorway. She looked
as stunned as he felt.

He drank in the sight of her. Her hair flowed down her
shoulders and her bright green printed dress hugged her
curves. But her beauty and glamour were downplayed.
He didn't know if that was by design or by mood. Had
she been suffering as much as him? Was it wrong that he
wanted her to share some of the heartache?

He marched over to Serena before she could react. He
needed to get to her before she shut the door between them
and hid. Not that it would stop him. He was prepared for
her to throw more obstacles in his way. He was ready to
tear down every barrier.

He hadn't seen her for over a month and the wait had
been agony. He wanted to chase her down and demand to
be heard but he knew it was not enough. He had to prove
that he was worthy of her trust and her love. He thought

he had done all he could and was ready to confront her. Now he wasn't so sure.

"What are you doing here?" Serena asked. He could see her throat tighten as he approached. "How did you find me?"

Cooper stood in front of her. He ached to touch her and hold her close. He felt the tremor in his fingers as he kept his hands to his sides. "I asked Felipe."

She jerked as if she'd been hit. "My father?" she asked hoarsely. "Leave him alone, Cooper. He can't handle another setback."

He frowned when he saw the hunted look in her golden-brown eyes. "Why do you automatically assume that I'm out to hurt him?" he asked in a low, fierce tone. "What do I have to do to prove that I'm not the enemy?"

She glanced around. The room was quiet and he felt all eyes on them. Serena muttered something in Portuguese before she ushered him inside her office. "Let's talk in private."

Relief and triumph squeezed his chest. It was a small victory but it was something he could build on. He stepped into the small room and the first thing he noticed were the white bookcases lining the raspberry-pink walls. The shelves were crammed with binders, business magazines and a few pieces of glass and ceramic art. He recognized the piece of pottery she had bought from the village in Portugal.

He walked to the dainty white desk in the center of the room. It was covered with stacks of reports and a slim silver laptop. Now this was the Serena he knew and loved. He could tell that this was her favorite spot in the world.

"What is it that you do here?" he asked as she closed the door.

"Didn't my father tell you?"

He shook his head. Felipe Dominguez had been vague about what his daughter did. Felipe had been more interested in getting Cooper to invest in his latest deal.

Serena leaned her hip against the corner of her desk. "This is a microfinance service for people in need. Right now I'm working with small-business owners who need loans but I plan to help individuals and families, as well."

Cooper was impressed that she had managed to get it up and running in very little time. He knew he shouldn't be surprised. Serena could accomplish anything with her intense focus. "Why?" he asked. "Why are you doing this?"

"Because I could have used something like this when I was in this neighborhood." Serena crossed her arms and looked out the window to a view of the crowded street. "The only thing that motivated me was the need for revenge. And I held on to that for too long."

Serena paused and her cheeks turned red. She kept looking out the window as if her life depended on it. "Someone once suggested I use my talents for something more meaningful."

Hope and pride swelled in his chest. He had said that to her. He had inspired her to do this. After everything that had happened between them, why did she follow his suggestion? Could she hate him while respecting his opinion?

Cooper gave a cursory glance at the analysis statements on her desk. He noticed that Serena's goal was ambitious. "How can you afford this?"

"I sold all of my jewelry."

Cooper felt a jolt of surprise and only then realized she wore no jewels. It was odd to see her ears and neck bare. She always wore something that caught the light or the attention. "Why would you do that? Didn't they have sentimental value?"

She shook her head. "I thought they did but I was

wrong. They had once belonged to my mother but she didn't want them anymore."

"They were your heritage," he pointed out. He remembered her talking about the awful feeling of selling off heirlooms.

"They were a piece of family history that I gave too much importance to," Serena said. "It was time to let them go."

"That's not going to be enough to keep this venture going."

"I'm expecting a very generous contribution from a very grateful businessman in London," she explained. "Now, why were you speaking to my father?"

He took a deep breath. "I'm the sole investor of his beachfront property idea."

"Fala sério," she whispered as her eyes widened in horror. She pressed her hands against her cheeks as her skin lost color. "You shouldn't have done that."

Cooper disagreed. "Yes, I should. Felipe lost everything because of my family fourteen years ago. He lost all of his investors again because of my father. Because of me," he amended. "I had to fix it."

"It's a risky idea, Cooper. All of my father's ideas are." She dragged her fingers down her face. "Yes, it might work but the chances aren't good."

"I'll make sure it works." Felipe needed someone to believe in him. Once the older man regained his confidence, he would not rely so heavily on Serena.

"How are you going to do that? Remember, he betrayed your father."

"He won't double-cross me." Cooper understood the intense pressure Felipe had suffered from Aaron Brock but he didn't agree with Felipe's actions. He knew the man was weak and had retaliated against the Brock empire because he had felt disrespected. Status was the most important thing to Felipe Dominguez and Cooper would indulge the man if it meant keeping Serena happy.

Serena pressed her hands together as if she were in prayer. "Cooper, I don't want you anywhere near my family. My parents have already suffered because of you and your father."

"And now it's my turn to protect them." Not just from Aaron Brock but from themselves. They had been a burden to Serena and he wanted to help her.

Serena pursed her lips. "I've seen your brand of protection."

"And I've seen yours. You protected me even when you said you were going to destroy me." Cooper took a step forward. "Why did you send me the file? Why didn't you use it like you threatened?"

Serena pushed away from the table and held her arms tighter against her body. "You proved to me that I was swimming with the sharks. I needed to get out of the game before I got hurt."

"That's not true." He slid his hand under her chin and tilted her face so she had to look at him. "You were holding your own just fine."

"No, I wasn't. I fell for your scam and didn't even realize it until it was too late."

"That was no scam, Serena," he said softly as his heart violently skipped a beat. "I'm in love with you."

This was the biggest risk he had ever made. He was declaring his love and hoped she could love him back. Prayed that she could find something inside him that was lovable.

He felt the tension arc through her body before she yanked away from him. "You need to leave," she said coldly.

Cooper stared at Serena's blank expression and something close to fear twisted inside him. "It's true."

"No, it's not."

How could he convince her? Panic began to claw at him. "I fell for you the minute I saw you at that charity dinner."

Her hand shook as she pointed at the door. "Get out right now."

Cooper knew he should cut his losses but he couldn't. He had to fight for her, for them. "And I'm still in love with you even when you're trying to stab me in the back."

Unshed tears glittered in her eyes. "*I* didn't betray *you*."

"I didn't ask my father to destroy your family! I always intended to keep my promise. You, however, were always going to use the information you had on my father," he accused as he watched Serena straighten her spine. "Even if it meant I got destroyed in the process. It was your insurance. Something you needed to use in case I went after you and your family."

"You did go after us." She tossed her hands in the air. "You were never going to let me go quietly."

"But you surprised me. You didn't use the information. Why?"

"You always knew that I didn't have the killer instinct. I couldn't bring myself to ruin a life. That's what you showed me in Portugal," she said quietly. "I didn't want to hear it but it was true. I was reluctant to let go of the revenge because it was the one constant in my life. But you showed me that I had to before it destroyed me."

Cooper didn't think he deserved the credit. Serena had saved herself.

"Why did you pull back when you could have destroyed the Dominguez family again?" she asked.

"You knew it was me." He often wondered if she had figured it out. She had refused to talk to him and he couldn't tell if she saw him as her guardian angel or as her nemesis.

"Of course it was you," she said. "You are the only one who could stop your father. By the time I flew to London to take care of my mother, the threats had stopped."

"I didn't know what my father was doing until you told me," Cooper insisted. "I wasn't part of that plan and I stopped it the moment I found out."

"Why did you bother? If you hadn't stepped in, I would have lost my influence in the financial world. No one would have listened to me if I told them about the information I had on Aaron or the truth about your first deal."

"Are you kidding me?" he asked in a raspy voice as shock rippled through him. "I did it to protect you. I will continue to protect you because you are mine, Serena. You always have been."

Serena slowly shook her head. "That's not true."

"At first I thought it was instant attraction," he admitted. "Pure lust or a strong connection. But it's more than that." Cooper rocked back on his feet as the heat washed over him. He knew nothing could link them as powerfully as what they shared now except for a baby.

He wanted to have children with this woman. Not heirs but children. A family. Share something that would bind them together more than vows and a ring. He hadn't considered becoming a father but the idea of having a family with Serena was irresistible.

"You're imagining things. Crazy things." She turned and walked to the door.

He speared his hands in his hair. "You've made me crazy. I can't sleep. I can't focus on work. I have found no peace. All I think about is you. Tell me you have been the same since you walked out on me."

Serena whirled on her heel and tilted her chin in the air. "I haven't given you a thought since I left Portugal."

He marched over to her. "I ache for you. So much that my skin stings for your touch."

She shivered. "I don't know what that feels like."

He grabbed her upper arms. He was so close to her and yet he felt so far away. "I don't know what to do to get you back. I want you to trust me. Love me. I want you to yearn to be with me. With every decision I make at work, I ask myself if you would be proud of me."

Confusion clouded her eyes. "Why?"

"Because you are everything to me," he said in a growl. "How can you not see it?"

"I thought... There was a moment when I believed it. When I—when we—were the only thing that mattered to you." She closed her eyes and swallowed hard. "But I was wrong," she whispered.

"No, you are my world," he said. "You know it and it scares the hell out of you."

She shook her head.

"That's why you ran," he continued. "It's why you refused to listen to me. You always need proof but not that time. You were so quick to believe I failed you. It's like you were waiting for it to happen."

"No, what we had was supposed to be temporary." She pressed her hands against his chest and tried to break free from his hold. "It didn't matter..."

"I'm not like the other people in your life, Serena. I will be there for you," he vowed. "I want to celebrate every big and small moment with you. I want to hold you close when you stumble and fall."

She took in a shaky breath. "What are you saying?"

"I am always going to support and protect you. Even

if you refuse to marry me. You are still mine and I will always be yours."

"Stop," she said weakly.

He couldn't. He needed Serena to understand. "I can't make you trust me. I may have ruined my chance for that to happen, but you need to know this. I trust you. You have my heart, my future, in your hands."

Her fingers curled against his jacket. "Don't do this."

"I am at your mercy," he admitted. His voice was raw and broken. "You have the power to destroy me. And I willingly give you that power."

Serena rested her head against his chest. "Why?"

"Because I trust you in ways I can't even explain." He gently cupped her head with his hands and guided her to look at him. "I know that when you're angry, when you think you hate me and you want to fight back, you won't hurt me. I trust you with everything I have and one day I hope you will learn to trust me."

"Cooper..."

"I love you, Serena. Let me back into your life," he pleaded. "Into your heart."

She pulled him closer. "You've been there all along."

* * * * *

If you enjoyed this book, look out
for the next installment of
THE CHATSFIELD:
CHATSFIELD'S ULTIMATE ACQUISITION
by Melanie Milburne
Coming next month.

MILLS & BOON®
Hardback – July 2015

ROMANCE

The Ruthless Greek's Return	Sharon Kendrick
Bound by the Billionaire's Baby	Cathy Williams
Married for Amari's Heir	Maisey Yates
A Taste of Sin	Maggie Cox
Sicilian's Shock Proposal	Carol Marinelli
Vows Made in Secret	Louise Fuller
The Sheikh's Wedding Contract	Andie Brock
Tycoon's Delicious Debt	Susanna Carr
A Bride for the Italian Boss	Susan Meier
The Millionaire's True Worth	Rebecca Winters
The Earl's Convenient Wife	Marion Lennox
Vettori's Damsel in Distress	Liz Fielding
Unlocking Her Surgeon's Heart	Fiona Lowe
Her Playboy's Secret	Tina Beckett
The Doctor She Left Behind	Scarlet Wilson
Taming Her Navy Doc	Amy Ruttan
A Promise...to a Proposal?	Kate Hardy
Her Family for Keeps	Molly Evans
Seduced by the Spare Heir	Andrea Laurence
A Royal Amnesia Scandal	Jules Bennett

MILLS & BOON®
Large Print – July 2015

ROMANCE

The Taming of Xander Sterne	Carole Mortimer
In the Brazilian's Debt	Susan Stephens
At the Count's Bidding	Caitlin Crews
The Sheikh's Sinful Seduction	Dani Collins
The Real Romero	Cathy Williams
His Defiant Desert Queen	Jane Porter
Prince Nadir's Secret Heir	Michelle Conder
The Renegade Billionaire	Rebecca Winters
The Playboy of Rome	Jennifer Faye
Reunited with Her Italian Ex	Lucy Gordon
Her Knight in the Outback	Nikki Logan

HISTORICAL

The Soldier's Dark Secret	Marguerite Kaye
Reunited with the Major	Anne Herries
The Rake to Rescue Her	Julia Justiss
Lord Gawain's Forbidden Mistress	Carol Townend
A Debt Paid in Marriage	Georgie Lee

MEDICAL

How to Find a Man in Five Dates	Tina Beckett
Breaking Her No-Dating Rule	Amalie Berlin
It Happened One Night Shift	Amy Andrews
Tamed by Her Army Doc's Touch	Lucy Ryder
A Child to Bind Them	Lucy Clark
The Baby That Changed Her Life	Louisa Heaton

MILLS & BOON®
Hardback – August 2015

ROMANCE

The Greek Demands His Heir	Lynne Graham
The Sinner's Marriage Redemption	Annie West
His Sicilian Cinderella	Carol Marinelli
Captivated by the Greek	Julia James
The Perfect Cazorla Wife	Michelle Smart
Claimed for His Duty	Tara Pammi
The Marakaios Baby	Kate Hewitt
Billionaire's Ultimate Acquisition	Melanie Milburne
Return of the Italian Tycoon	Jennifer Faye
His Unforgettable Fiancée	Teresa Carpenter
Hired by the Brooding Billionaire	Kandy Shepherd
A Will, a Wish...a Proposal	Jessica Gilmore
Hot Doc from Her Past	Tina Beckett
Surgeons, Rivals...Lovers	Amalie Berlin
Best Friend to Perfect Bride	Jennifer Taylor
Resisting Her Rebel Doc	Joanna Neil
A Baby to Bind Them	Susanne Hampton
Doctor...to Duchess?	Annie O'Neil
Second Chance with the Billionaire	Janice Maynard
Having Her Boss's Baby	Maureen Child

MILLS & BOON®
Large Print – August 2015

ROMANCE

The Billionaire's Bridal Bargain	Lynne Graham
At the Brazilian's Command	Susan Stephens
Carrying the Greek's Heir	Sharon Kendrick
The Sheikh's Princess Bride	Annie West
His Diamond of Convenience	Maisey Yates
Olivero's Outrageous Proposal	Kate Walker
The Italian's Deal for I Do	Jennifer Hayward
The Millionaire and the Maid	Michelle Douglas
Expecting the Earl's Baby	Jessica Gilmore
Best Man for the Bridesmaid	Jennifer Faye
It Started at a Wedding...	Kate Hardy

HISTORICAL

A Ring from a Marquess	Christine Merrill
Bound by Duty	Diane Gaston
From Wallflower to Countess	Janice Preston
Stolen by the Highlander	Terri Brisbin
Enslaved by the Viking	Harper St. George

MEDICAL

A Date with Her Valentine Doc	Melanie Milburne
It Happened in Paris...	Robin Gianna
The Sheikh Doctor's Bride	Meredith Webber
Temptation in Paradise	Joanna Neil
A Baby to Heal Their Hearts	Kate Hardy
The Surgeon's Baby Secret	Amber McKenzie

MILLS & BOON®

Why shop at millsandboon.co.uk?

Each year, thousands of romance readers find their perfect read at millsandboon.co.uk. That's because we're passionate about bringing you the very best romantic fiction. Here are some of the advantages of shopping at www.millsandboon.co.uk:

* **Get new books first**—you'll be able to buy your favourite books one month before they hit the shops

* **Get exclusive discounts**—you'll also be able to buy our specially created monthly collections, with up to 50% off the RRP

* **Find your favourite authors**—latest news, interviews and new releases for all your favourite authors and series on our website, plus ideas for what to try next

* **Join in**—once you've bought your favourite books, don't forget to register with us to rate, review and join in the discussions

Visit **www.millsandboon.co.uk**
for all this and more today!